STRANGERS
NO MORE

Word Association Publishers
205 Fifth Avenue
Tarentum, Pennsylvania 15084
www.wordassociation.com.
1.800.827.7903

Strangers No More

Layout and Design by Jason Price & Lloyd Stamy

Publisher's Cataloging-In-Publication Data

Stamy, Lloyd F. Jr., 1951-
Strangers no more / by Lloyd Stamy
Tarentum, Pennsylvania : Word Association Publishers, 2021. |
A Hap Franklin novel ; [2]

ISBN 978-1-63385-416-1
Library of Congress Control Number: 2021903537

LCSH: Espionage--Fiction. | Romance--Fiction--American |
Russia--Foreign relations--United States--Fiction | China--Foreign economic
relations--United States--Fiction | Corruption--Fiction. | Election Cyber
Security--United States--Fiction. | LCGFT: Spy fiction.
LCC PS374.S764 S77 2021 | DDC 813/.6--dc23

STRANGERS
NO MORE

LLOYD STAMY

CONTENTS

DEDICATION

To my loving and precious daughter and son, Caroline and Jonathan—both God-given daily blessings to whom this book is dedicated—I apologize for the mess my generation has left this world in and for you to cope with, but know you will be far better stewards of the planet and all life that struggles to coexist here in harmony.

Good luck, stay happy, and savor the wonder of life while ignoring its noise. As you would expect from me, here's yet another list—an additional baker's dozen of life's lessons to embrace.

- Keep smiling.
- Follow your dreams.
- Remain in love.
- Continue to learn and think.
- Do your best, and never settle for less.
- Live large.
- Nourish your faith.
- Be charitable.
- Make your mark in life (and punctuate it with an exclamation point when necessary).
- Have conviction.
- Stay vigilant.
- And above all, work hard, but have some fun along the way.

All my love,
Daddy

FOREWORD

As with any sequel or follow-on novel, it's always better to approach the work by first understanding the predecessor story to become familiar with its background. In this case, I believe it even more so and therefore encourage you to read *Reunion of Strangers* before turning another page of this book.

Because so many of you enjoyed the characters enough to demand that I follow them through life's next phase, that is what I've tried to do with *Strangers No More*. It is, however, difficult to do them justice and convey the full essence of their personalities and history through only the occasional throwback reference. Heeding this advice will enhance your enjoyment, I promise.

I am again indebted to the usual cast of characters who cajoled me along in this effort, and they know who they are. Worthy of special note were the efforts of editor, Martin McHugh, whose diligence, vigilance, and tenacity (particularly when arm wrestling over commas and the subjunctive mood) were appreciated. Fortunately, it was virtually impossible to hide the occasional dangling modifier from his hawk-eyed review.

Beyond those abiding friendships, I am especially grateful for the work of Mary Burns Holmes, a brilliant illustrator, creative artisan, and gifted artist who designed and painted the compelling book cover and interior illustrations accompanying each of the six major sections. Also, I salute Jason Price at Word Association Publishers for assembling all the pieces with aplomb while enduring my obsessions over the final package.

Last, I treasure the enduring connection with my longtime friend and literary muse who initially inspired the fanciful composite character and heroine known as Weezie.

As with all previous works, any proceeds (author commissions and royalties) earned from the publication of this book will be donated to charity.

—LLOYD F. STAMY, JR., *February, 2021*

PRELUDE:
COMMITMENT AT THE CROSSROADS

T HERE HAD BEEN A MAGNETIC AND MAGICAL DYNAMIC between them since the seventh grade, but it had taken decades for them to act on it. Once they had, there was no turning back despite the unforeseen risks of discovery and danger. After two years of grieving over the death of his wife, Hap was inexorably drawn to the broken shards of his life's unfinished business, and Louise was atop that list.

From the start, Louise was hauntingly seductive without ever trying to be so. She had never been the kind of gal who put on the dog to attract attention, and that was probably because she never needed to. As opposed to the packaging, it was the inner core of her being that was so enchanting. Her scintillating appeal was centered in wholesomeness despite its all too frequent result of bringing about an acute case of teenage tendonitis in the morning. Nowadays, the only risk from their relationship would more likely be a coronary event. When Louise lost her own way over the years, she had always found a way back and now was equally determined to help show Hap the way home too.

When taking time to stare deeply into the mirror, Hap realized he could become a basket case without her. He couldn't figure out why such musings about her occurred when he was alone and at rest, but perhaps it was because that was when the nightmares took over and he was most vulnerable.

The legacy of a life spent in overdrive was one that Hap understood, but he was unable to embrace its inevitable consequences. The problem was that the endgame had turned out to be not nearly as satisfying as it had once promised. He spent important years chasing success, but in the recesses of his mind, he feared he might never be satisfied in the ways he had always hoped to be. It was time for him to get life right before the curtain. There was a time when only he and God knew how difficult that path would be for a man so resistant to change. The game changer was that Louise had discovered that too.

As had always been the case, it didn't take long for Hap's game plan to be interrupted, and once again, he was thrown back into the same firestorm from which he had been desperately trying to escape. This time, it was an unfamiliar but foreboding cross-roads that served only to further stoke his resolve. The long-running American experiment with democracy was in jeopardy of collapsing by all manner of domestic and Russian interference. Even more devastating was the longer-term threat of permanent economic enslavement by China.

Because the country needed him now more than ever before, Louise and his retirement would have to be put on the back burner. Though his was a complicated past desperately in need of closure, the allure of Louise and siren call to preserve democracy were irresistible.

PART I:
Overture

A PREEMPTIVE STRIKE

HAD HAP BEEN MORE ALERT, he may have seen it coming, but he wasn't … and didn't. The incendiary missile exploded with such ferocity that the earth shook and he was immediately knocked to the ground. A second later, the sky was ablaze from the apparent self-destruction of a military drone that had successfully delivered its payload. Despite covering his ears, Hap was deafened by the concussive aftershocks from the two blasts. The target, once Hap's home, was in smoky ruins. Instead of barking, his dog, Bailey, huddled in the farthest corner of the fenced-in garden unable to understand what had happened and wanting no part in it.

Three more successive explosions erupted, which Hap guessed were the gas tanks of the cars in the garage exploding. The devastation was complete. A shower of dust and debris rained over the grounds, meaning that any evidence from the drone that might have helped trace its origin had been all but vaporized. Of course, none of that would be necessary; the source was unmistakable. Hap knew what had happened. It was all too obvious. Promises had been broken, a deal had been made, and Dmitri Cherkov was still alive and back in the game.

The drone must have had good eyes as it had launched its projectile only after Hap had reached the garden—a safe distance from the house and far enough away to escape injury. Such synchrony meant somewhere, someone with insider insight was in command. Hap instinctively grasped the intended message—he had been kept out of harm's way and deliberately saved for another day. Louise had left for Baltimore only minutes before, so the plan was that she too would be purposefully distanced far from the kill zone.

Like a shot over the bow, the assault was only a warning of what might follow. This opening salvo signaled the ascendancy of Cherkov's return to power with a brazen display of ego, and it announced that no one was beyond his reach even when on American soil. Hap was all too familiar with such classic, psychological warfare, and the sadistic drama surrounding this outrageous action bore the outright distinction of Cherkov's fingerprints.

The police chief, with both patrol cars in close chase behind him, arrived within minutes and well ahead of the fire trucks. Hap knew from the chief's demeanor that all this stuff involving the clandestine side of Hap's life was really pissing him off. Nothing was said until the two officers began examining the wreckage and were well out of earshot. The chief just stared at Hap awaiting the explanation he knew wouldn't be forthcoming, or if so, would be far from the truth. To do so convincingly, Hap would have to buck it up and keep the chief off balance by summoning his usual brand of panache. It was time to put on his mask of confidence to cover up the omnipresent self-doubt hidden just underneath. If not, the chief would surely see that Hap's customary twinkling eyes belied the emotionless, stone-cold stare of a killer. Hap's ears hadn't yet stopped ringing, and he could barely hear what came from his own mouth. Though audible, even the timbre of his voice was unfamiliar over the thunderous pounding of what he expected would be a prolonged and painful headache.

"Well Chief, I suppose you'll have to make that call again."

"Oh you bet I will, Mr. Franklin, just as soon as we determine what's happened here and that all is safe and sound. In the meantime, your minders at Langley will have to wait. What was that spook's name? Bud, wasn't it?"

"Good memory, Chief. It was Bud—Bud Smith—and just between us, he's a big cheese there now."

"And just so you know, I'm not about to be cowered into submission again."

"Chief, you've gotta stay in your own lane on this one."

"Your buddy Bud may be CIA or God knows what else, but this happened here on soil under my watch, so I'm taking charge this time."

"I'm afraid you're gonna be disappointed … again."

Many years earlier, the chief had been officially tasked by much higher law enforcement powers in DC to immediately alert a guy named Bud if Hap or his family was in any kind of danger. This was certainly one of those times. He had done so only once before, when Hap's wife, Kate, had perished in a suspicious crash that had all but incinerated her car. The day's audacious airstrike was well beyond that, and it would be up to the chief to fashion and release a plausible cover story for public consumption. Only then would the unvarnished truth be reported up the chain of command to the boys in black at Langley.

The blaring sirens of the fire trucks were getting louder. Due to its mostly stone and masonry construction, there wasn't too much remaining of Hap's home that would require the fire brigade's attention. When the hook and ladder crew began pulling hose, Hap told them not to waste the water. Given his Pennsylvania Dutch heritage and penchant for thrift, it seemed an appropriate response.

"Let's not give up on it yet, Mr. Franklin. There may be some things we can save."

"No, let it burn—they're only charred artifacts now. My life in Fox Chapel has come to an end, and there's no salvage value in anything here—only memories … some good, some bad."

Hap knew what he had said was bullshit before the words had finished escaping his mouth. Recalling the derogatory and overworn expression "Once a chappie, always a chappie" from his youth, he knew that long-standing axiom overrode his comments. Seeing the look of suspicion on their faces confirmed it because that was precisely what the firemen were thinking too but wouldn't dare say. Up in smoke was not the way they would provide this homegrown chappie a convenient way out.

The chief also kept silent; he too knew better and wasn't buying it. After all, this was the place where Hap Franklin had grown up and still called home; abandoning it at that point was not in the cards. The expansive file on Hap kept under lock back at the station was the thickest of any resident, and the chief was privy to a wealth of additional classified information unknown to others. He knew the stuff Hap was made from and was capable of, and he had previously witnessed the danger he could attract. Despite Hap's low public profile and overall likeableness, the chief considered him a self-made, self-styled, and apparently self-governed man, all of which made him a risk to maintaining the usual tranquility folks found appealing about the borough of Fox Chapel.

It wasn't long before choppers from the television stations took their turns hovering overhead to get footage for their next broadcasts. Hap dreaded what he figured would be the headline, "Fiery Explosion Levels One of Fox Chapel's Largest Estates." Local news content was always driven by the sensational instead of the really important narratives of the day, which to Hap made stories like this rather pedestrian despite all the hoopla. But the stations had ratings to uphold, and they somehow believed they could boost them by satisfying the near-prurient curiosity of their rabid viewers.

The chief's phone and radio rang incessantly, but reflectively awash in thought, he answered neither. He was not the kind of flatfoot who was ever caught flat-footed, so he took his time silently rehearsing the charade until he was ready to offer a measured response of carefully parsed comments. Since the explosion was already being reported by the media as the result of a suspected gas leak, that was the scenario the chief decided to go with when eventually asked for confirmation.

ASHEN REMNANTS

O NLY AFTER HIS PRELIMINARY INSPECTION was made could the chief make a threat assessment. Once he determined there was no imminent danger beyond the fire, he told the firemen they could go. His job was to protect and defend all the borough residents, not just Hap's immediate neighborhood, so it was important to him that all under his care would sleep soundly that night. But he wasn't yet ready to issue such assurances for the future until after he'd made a call to Bud Smith at the untraceable number that didn't formally exist.

Fox Chapel was one of those special places reserved only for inhabitants of privilege. All big cities and particularly the once-mighty industrial ones had such exclusionary suburbs, but few were like this one, which was outside Pittsburgh. It was swanky yet intentionally understated. More than a century earlier, much of the land had been set aside permanently in a land trust to protect the mature forests so the breathtaking landscape would remain pristine and unspoiled by overdevelopment. Such long-term initiatives could have occurred only with thoughtful foresight and would never have happened without the substantial means its residents enjoyed. Some like Hap had made their own ways in life through sheer hard work driven by self-determination. Others included third- and fourth-generation idle rich who had only marked time while nursing from the bosom of family trust funds established long ago by former titans of the Industrial Revolution.

The reason for the chief's success in such a place was simple—his daily pledge of allegiance was to keep all of them safe, and he had done a good job until the near back-to-back incidents involving Hap Franklin.

"What else can we do for you, Mr. Franklin?"

"Nothing, really. There's a pickup in the stable, and my cell phone is fully charged."

"But where will you sleep?"

"I'll figure that out later, but probably the barn. All I really need to do is run out for some dog food to keep the hound happy."

"Okay, but you'll call if you need anything, right? My patrolmen will swing by throughout the day and tonight to keep an eye on the place."

Hap knew of course that the chief really meant keeping an eye on him.

Once the police cruisers and fire trucks had gone, Hap just sat down, head in hands, where he had been before it all had begun several hours earlier—the limestone bench he had designed after seeing a similar one in the garden of Leonardo da Vinci's final home in the Loire Valley. After taking such a sucker punch from his Russian nemesis, Hap knew its crippling effect would not soon wear off. But it was not the time for maudlin sentimentality; besides, there was no longer any vodka to help such thoughts along and only the dog to keep him company. Reluctantly, he decided to take a closer look at what if anything remained of his home. Before that inspection, he returned to the garden to comfort the dog, which had remained crouched and cowering in silence until Hap patiently coaxed him from hiding.

The few thin threads of white smoke curling in the light breeze offered proof that some parts of the house were still smoldering. Fire always took a longer time to extinguish than most onlookers would expect, and this one was no different. Hap had to restrain himself from rummaging through the ashes too soon, which in a perverse way was more annoying than the devastation itself. He knew the sight of the fire would forever be scorched into his optic nerves as a painful reminder of this day and the arrogance of the perpetrator. As anyone else would, he wanted to cry, but he couldn't.

Most of the house was no longer distinguishable. The only remnant that remained intact was the secret bunker and the items stored in it—his stack of passports, weaponry of all kinds, a vast trove of surveillance gear, ceramic-plated body armor, some currency and bars of gold bullion, a fresh burner phone, and the all-important go bag.

He was pretty sure that the lead-lined and battle-armored steel safe room had done its job. Curiously, it dawned on Hap that what remained of his life was limited to the tools of his former tradecraft in that room. Perhaps this duplicitous residue of his past also signaled that Hap was being called back to a place from which he had only recently escaped. Aware that too often such clandestine lifestyles had destroyed other men, he was not about to let that happen. Before the day's events, he had hoped to be unhitched from the CIA for good, but at that point, he yearned to be put back in harness once more.

He realized there was one corollary albeit unintentional benefit of Cherkov's disintegration of the Franklin family home. That solitary silver lining was that Hap had been saved from having to grapple with what he had long dreaded, an inevitable and painful chore. Kate and Hap had hung onto stuff for far too long, never having worked up the courage to jettison what had become a veritable warehouse of keepsakes long past their expiration dates. More than most folks, they knew that stuff was valuable only if it reminded them of someone they loved, which beyond their son and daughter included their extended families. He wished he'd had the chance to go through it all one last time, but he knew what remained in the bunker was all he might need to avenge the wrong.

Because of Cherkov's unprovoked assault, Hap had a final score to settle, and given his bloodlust, he needed to make sure it happened in a big way. The explosion underscored that it would never be over between them until one was dead. The finality of such an ending was not something he feared but actually looked forward to, as long as he was the victor rather than the victim. After all, the only reliable way to cheat death was to stay alive.

While wading through the ashes, he nearly tripped over the cast-iron weights from one of his favorite possessions—a tall case clock from the colonial period that had been in his family for five generations. Nearby, he saw the clock's hand-painted metal face and picked it up for a final look. He once had a prized collection of working antique timepieces—French table clocks, early American mantel clocks, and English grandfather clocks. All had been in perfect working order, and over the heated protests of Kate and the kids because of the ruckus they made when striking the hour at the same time, Hap had always made sure they were hand-wound on a weekly basis.

The sole structure still standing was the remote stable, which no longer housed any horses but rather unimportant things including a tractor, an old Ford pickup, two canoes, an abundance of tools, an assortment of landscaping equipment, and enough camping gear to equip a platoon. Though it had been nothing but a warehouse in recent years, Hap still enjoyed spending quiet time there and listening to the creaking of the copper weathervane atop the cupola moving with the breeze.

He stretched out on the old couch he had moved there years ago for enjoying the infrequent downtime between the frenzied parts of his life. Sometimes, he had needed such intermissions if only to keep his two lives apart and straight in his mind. Additional creature comfort was provided by a stereo system with several big-ass speakers he had installed for listening to sixties music that Kate couldn't abide being played in the house. Only when she was away had he been able to flip on all twelve home speakers, crank the volume up, and rock the whole place. Other times required that he take refuge in the stable, where the music wouldn't drive her as crazy. He wasn't fooling anyone when he disappeared there, and least of all Kate, because in the house, it still sounded like a live performance by the Beatles but heard outside Shea Stadium.

Hearing that concert from the parking lot was an experience Hap had never forgotten even after half a century. Too young to drive in 1966, he and his friend Mac had defied their parents by taking a Greyhound to New York, believing they could somehow get in without tickets. They didn't, and thus had been relegated to listening from a parking lot several hundred yards away, but that was a secret they'd kept from everyone else. Thereafter, they would describe the Fab Four experience in a way that nobody would have ever known that they hadn't had front-row seats. Of course, both were grounded for the remainder of the summer once they found their way home. Worse yet, their weekly allowances were suspended for the rest of the year and their chores were doubled. Fortunately, the experience didn't keep them from trying it all over again three years later by hitchhiking to Woodstock, where tickets weren't required.

The stable's other attraction was the scent—a mixture of hay, manure, sawdust, and saddlery. Unlike those expensive, noxious ones that came from a perfume bottle, these smells were the honest ones that Hap enjoyed the most. Though the stalls had been mucked out years earlier when the horses were sold, the faint, sweet aroma of manure still lingered. Hap thought that the persistence of the odors was another way Mother Nature asserted her dominion and rightful sovereignty. He and his son, Christian, had spent good times cleaning their riding boots and the tack with saddle soap and then softening the leather with hand-rubbed neat's-foot oil until it glistened. It was there too that they had designed and built the blue-ribbon winner of the Cub Scout pinewood derby.

Beyond the saddlery, another relic gathering dust was his daughter's racing shell that hung from the rafters. Her name, Lindsay, had been discreetly painted in script along both sides of the single scull's bow. It was a thing of beauty especially when seen cutting its way upstream through the swift current of the Allegheny River. Hap recalled the joy of her victories and his angst when Lindsay got too close to the Highland Park Dam, certain she'd go over and perish.

Much like the StairMaster, the elliptical, the rowing machine, the ergometer, the recumbent bike, the punching bag, and the weights in the exercise room, the gleaming shell hadn't seen much use for many years. The stable was never intended to be its final place of mooring. Given that the scull cost more than most cars, Hap knew he should have donated it to the crew team as he had planned. However, he had found it hard to give up the comfort and fond memories its presence evoked even when suspended in time and in the wrong place. Since it was too soon to let go of those and other recollections, Hap wasn't prepared to leave the stable just yet, so this was where he and Bailey would spend the night. It probably wasn't the right choice, but Hap had his own idiosyncratic way of dealing with most everything.

He had much to reflect on, especially the missed opportunities for which he had only himself to blame. It wasn't the first time he had tasted loneliness, and he still found it a bitter flavor. Since time was something he might soon be running out of, he knew that seeking his son's and daughter's forgiveness for Kate's death was something he could no longer postpone. He also worried that perhaps his calcified heart had gotten too hard for any repentance. Unburdening himself would demand sharing more with them than he should. Nevertheless, they were entitled to the whole story, and only he could tell it. Despite its being heavily redacted, he knew that the CIA's official file would never be released to anyone, so he vowed to remain alive long enough to tell them the truth.

Suddenly, his thoughts were interrupted by an incoming message that appeared simultaneously as a text and an email.

"Franklin, your house was just the beginning, comrade. Eventually, I will take everything from you. You will soon learn what it's like to be totally fucked, but unlike me, there will be no escape for you. Cherkov."

The message slowly dissolved as the screen went dark. A moment later, the phone began shutting itself down without any prompting. Though not encrypted like the one he had used when undercover, this one, his personal cell phone, had never been hacked before. It had all the latest detection and avoidance software to maintain his anonymity and privacy. The breach meant Cherkov must have had access to the most robust malware available. Invasive snooping was one thing, but having the ability to close Hap down and shut him out from all electronic communication was more than problematic. He clearly would need all of Langley's sophisticated tools of tradecraft before moving forward.

THAT'S NO WAY TO SAY GOODBYE

L OUISE, OR WEEZIE AS SHE WAS KNOWN by her friends, would be expecting his call to make sure she had arrived home safely. Hap knew it was imperative that he not betray any hint of the devastation that had just occurred or the anxiety it caused. As a brilliant behavioral psychologist, she could almost smell angst and apprehension, so he had to be extra careful. Once emotionally prepared for the masquerade, and using the burner phone retrieved from the safe room, he phoned, and she answered on the first ring.

"Hello, and who's this?"

"It's your buddy Hap."

"Oh. I didn't recognize the number, and there was no caller ID, but hey, it's about time you checked in."

"My phone is down for the count, so I'll be using this spare one for a while. So how was the drive to Baltimore? Your car should know the way by now, so I figured you flipped on the autopilot and took a nap."

"I'm home, unpacked, and with appropriate gratitude to you am now soaking my weary body in a hot bath with a glass of wine."

"Let me guess—a buttery Chardonnay?"

"I like a man who already knows all the answers to his questions."

"I'm a quick study and often clairvoyant. Oh and by the way, unlike you, I'm not stiff at all."

"Well you were, Hap, and nearly all weekend."

Of course he had been, and he had ended up utterly fatigued after their marathon, but he obviously hadn't had time to relax and work out the kinks since her departure. They had made a practice of alternating locations for their weekly visits, and the next would be at her home, so although taken aback, Hap was also relieved when Weezie continued.

"Oh Hap, before I forget, and I'm so sorry to break the news to you over the phone, but I must revoke your conjugal visitation rights next week."

"What? Why? Don't tell me you need more R&R to fully recoup after being here?"

"In your dreams, Romeo. Truthfully, after reviewing my already full schedule, I'll need the weekend to finish that paper for submission before the Brussels conference."

"But your conference isn't for another month, and we leave for Italy in two weeks."

"Don't worry. We'll work it out."

"Good, because I'd like to work it in too."

"And so you shall, and if you're good, maybe more than once. Now let me get back to my bath in order to be extra lithe and limber for you next time."

"Okay, but first, one more thing. Another class reunion's coming up, so we'd better begin thinking that through too. After all, as you'll remember, we were elected by acclamation to take it on again."

"Oh Jesus, Hap. There's no fucking way."

"Good grief, woman, curb that tongue. You sound like a stormtrooper off his meds."

"Oh that's right. I'd forgotten you're used to gentle language from genteel women—the kind spoken by those southern belles you couldn't get enough of at UVA."

"I like propriety, and if you, m'lady, ever want to be admitted to the Colonial Dames of America, you'd best leave sinning and swearing to the men."

"Since I know you're a card-carrying member of the Sons of the American Revolution, what do you suggest I do to make proper amends for dropping the F-bomb?"

"Well, as a favor, and only this one time, I could take you over my knee for a good spanking, but given your other sins of sexual misbehavior, it would have to be a bare-bottomed one."

"As punishment for premarital fornication or to satisfy another of your peccadilloes?"

"Just old-fashioned behavior modification, the kind you docs frown on these days."

"Nowadays, we recommend only the carrot approach, never the stick."

"Why not a little of both?"

"Not a bad idea, Hap, but here's another suggestion—When you're here next time, why don't you bend me over my kitchen table instead?"

For once, Hap was speechless. His puckish smile was followed by an uncontrollable guffaw. After joining him in laughter, Weezie couldn't help but ask, "So the indefatigable Benjamin Harrison Franklin is finally rendered mute and unable to get in the last word?"

"Never too stymied for a retort, my dear. Just remind me to check the legs of that table for stability and durability before I administer your comeuppance."

"It's time for me to get back to my bath, so let's say goodnight."

"Hey, that's no way to say goodbye."

"It is when I'm all hot and bothered."

"Then by all means I'll leave you to stew in your own juices even knowing it's no fair reawakening those desire over the phone."

"Besides me, Hap, is there anyone else who knows how good you are at being bad?"

"I try not to show my true colors with others. It's all part of the skullduggery."

"Oh how I know."

It was a good thing Weezie could not see his face, which bore the telltale signs of relief that she had no clue about what was troubling him. Hap figured there was no reason to tell her about the explosion and little chance she'd learn about it before he could explain. He was not about to give her one more thing to worry about, especially for fear she might jump to the right conclusion. Not having to make the road trip to Baltimore was a blessing and would give him more time to figure out what the right response should be to Cherkov's threat. Equally important was that he would get to see Weezie one more time before any real shit hit the fan.

CHARTING THE COURSE

ARMED WITH ONLY HIS INSTINCTS FOR SURVIVAL, Hap began forging a strategy for revenge. He was prepared to go it alone, but he thought that that might prove to be a fool's errand. Going it alone would be like charting a course without a compass. Using the resources of the CIA that were at his disposal was the only surefire way to have any chance of success. He also knew from experience that impatient hunters eventually became the hunted, and he would need more than arrows in his quiver when up against a savage like Cherkov.

As unnatural and unfamiliar as pleading was for him, he decided to make a pilgrimage to Langley, hoping it would be his last, and beg for Bud's help. Painful as it would be, swallowing his pride was preferable to taking a bullet, or worse, whatever else Cherkov might have in store for him. He also knew from experience that the problem with standing down in the face of the enemy made it nearly impossible to stand back up.

Hap hadn't picked this fight, but it was now up to him to finish it. Though he had done his part two years earlier by bringing Cherkov to the threshold of justice, someone had reneged on the promise to take him down. As always, the CIA had done its job to capture and interrogate the bastard. If left to them, Cherkov would have met his maker immediately thereafter, so the decision to spare his life must have been made farther up the food chain. That left two choices—the State Department or the commander in chief himself.

Getting at the truth would begin with Bud Smith since he had promised Hap that Cherkov would never again see the light of day. Bud had become the deputy director for operations, or DOD, but their relationship had been forged several decades before. It was Bud who had recruited Hap and later became his handler before ascending the ladder to overseeing all clandestine ops.

Though Hap had been reluctant when first approached by Bud twenty-odd years earlier about a special, part-time arrangement in service to the country, Bud had persisted and eventually prevailed, but Hap had somehow known from the start that it was his destiny. He knew that because of Hap's smarts, personality, and familiarity with most of the world, he could be an ideal agent. Hap's global personal and business travel had provided the perfect cover. During the extended recruitment process, Bud had gone as far as to enlist the unprecedented help of a sitting president who had once been the CIA's director. That Oval Office meeting was the big boost that sealed the deal; Hap found it impossible to turn down an offer from a president who was not only a very gifted closer but who also drank vodka martinis and did so with Hap after securing his commitment.

After a surprisingly restful sleep in the old, battered couch next to his dog in the barn, Hap figured it was time to bring Bud into the fold. He dialed the number every agent knew by heart— the one beginning with an area code that couldn't be found in any phone book. After being rerouted to a variety of places throughout the globe, it was answered in terse fashion by a woman.

"Password?"

"Cavalier," Hap answered.

She read a sentence and asked him to repeat it verbatim, which he did.

"Voice recognition verified. How can I help you?"

"Bud Smith, please. It's urgent."

"Right away, Cavalier."

Many stories about Hap's cloak-and-dagger missions, which continued to circulate through the ranks, had taken on lives of their own. Without his being there to confirm or refute their authenticity, some of the lore surrounding Hap Franklin had become downright apocryphal. Even absent the overblown hype, Hap's daring was legendary, and everyone knew that, including the operator answering the encrypted phone line.

Despite Hap's request for a quick connect to the DOD, he waited for what seemed an eternity until Bud came on the line. The delay, Hap figured, had been likely intentional. Beyond irritating Hap, it also gave their supercomputers time to trace and pinpoint the location of the caller.

"Why Hap, I'd expected your call before now, and before you start ripping me a new asshole, do know that I've been working on nothing else since your police chief called me last night."

"Cut the crap, Bud. Given that we both know who's responsible, I'd expect nothing less. Now how about the apology I'm sure you've rehearsed a dozen times while waiting for my call."

"As to your home, I really am sorry, but insofar as allowing Cherkov to live and reinvent himself, that wasn't my call. After we finished with him, his fate was in the hands of others well above me."

"Dammit! You promised me he'd never again be a threat to me, my kids, or Louise."

"Easy now, Hap. Let's dial it back a bit, okay? Frankly, I'm a little surprised at your temper as you're typically as unflappable a character as they come."

"Not when it involves being left out there naked in the dark. And what do you mean reinvented?"

"Cherkov's more powerful now than he had been. Following a good horsewhipping by the Russian president once we released him, they kissed and made up. After all, he was always the most successful oligarch, and his fealty to the czar was measured by an ongoing avalanche of rubles and cryptocurrencies."

"But you said reinvented."

"We hear he's had a complete makeover with a new cover, name, and even face. Apparently, we didn't grab all his dough as he didn't start from scratch. Beyond being bankrolled by the czar, he had to have had access to much more to rebuild what he has. My hunch is that most of his fortune was well concealed when we confiscated what we could get our hands on."

"So we're back to square one?"

"Hap, *you're* not back to anything. This is a company matter, and you're retired now."

"Maybe as a sanctioned agent, but once a spy, always a spy. You've said that yourself. For Christ's sake, Bud, don't you see it? I'm your only way in."

"Just take your vacation and cool off. I can protect you in Italy."

"How'd you know about that?"

"Unlike most employers, we're more like a big extended family here, Hap, and one with no secrets. More to the point, we like to keep close tabs on our retirees in case any might be thinking about wandering off the reservation and crossing over. For the record, you should know that all who have are now pushing up daisies."

"That's hardly in my nature, and you know it."

"Of course I do, but in your case, I'm more worried about your trying to even an old score and maybe singlehandedly, which would be foolish. Listen up for once—You can't go rogue and desperado on this one, Hap. You'll need plenty of resources and my help. If not, Cherkov will crush you in a way you can't begin to imagine."

"So I'm in?"

"Only if you play nice, but you'll remain an outsider, and any role you play will be completely off book."

"Why off book, Bud?"

"Unilateral decisions around here are applauded only when they're successful, so I'm gonna need plenty of room for deniability on this one if it goes south. Plus, I have just so much latitude under the current director. Secrecy, and especially on this one, is essential, and surveillance being our trade, I have my own people sweep this office for bugs every day. Some here—the director included—don't believe or have forgotten that loose lips sink ships."

Hap knew that Bud's paranoia was understandable. Beyond the general public, even federal employees had a rightful suspicion of government and especially in recent years. Outright distrust of all presidential appointees had become commonplace under the current administration. Some, like Bud, worried more about the enemy within than the ones they were intended to fight. As was the case with the FBI, directors at the CIA were replaced one by one at the whim of the commander in chief until he found a candidate who saluted his personal flag ahead of the starred and striped one. All arrived ready to heel, and most proved to be not much beyond shills meant to advance the administration's perplexing agenda.

Under any other leader, the normal and expected role of those in clandestine services would be straightforward. Following intensive intelligence collection, analyses were provided routinely to those who used it to craft foreign policy. But the sitting president didn't understand the art of geopolitical conflict, and he found his largely unread daily briefing papers of little strategic value.

Another risk to Bud was that though Cherkov's suspected but unverified activities seemed to demand an actionable response, he couldn't take the decision any higher. Given that the perpetrator was Cherkov with the probable assistance of the Russian president, a swift interdiction was appropriate. Usually, such intel would be shared with and blessed by the White House, but that place had become a virtual sieve when it came to sensitive information. Secrets told there were rarely kept, and typically leaked to a single favorite media outlet known for broadcasting without prior vetting.

There was another obstacle. Due to growing public antipathy, espionage was no longer the darling it once had been. Mainstream and private networks of all stripes were itching for any opportunity to put a bad face on the dark world where Bud operated, and he didn't like being compromised especially from his blind side. Nevertheless, launching this operation was imperative, and with Hap aboard, he felt comfortable greenlighting the initiative himself.

"So Hap, assuming you get my drift, are we understood?"

"I suppose."

"Then welcome home. I'll get back to you once you and the good doctor are back from Italy. We'll run some limited surveillance to make sure you're okay but nothing intrusive that might spoil your holiday."

"Wait. I'll need some things beforehand."

"Like what?"

"Standard-issue tools of the trade—a reliable encrypted cell phone, some combat gear, and untraceable fresh passports for both of us, but they have to be in our real names. I don't want to alert Weezie in any way of the possible peril in our path."

"Okay, I'll have the boys in ops put a suitcase of your favorite toys together. They know your preferences. The falsified replacement passports will take a bit longer. Ones with new identities would be far easier you know."

"Just do it, Bud. I have my reasons, but I don't want to discuss them over the phone, even on a line that's supposedly as secure as this one is."

"Maybe you'd better come in for a face to face."

"I thought you'd never ask."

"I'm almost afraid to ask, Hap, but is there anything else?"

"There is. I'd like private air transport to and from DC along with a brief stop at my place on the Chesapeake."

"You know damn well we can't get one of our birds anywhere near St. Michaels, and why do you need to go there anyway?"

"Since my entire wardrobe went up in smoke here, I'll need to pack some old but recognizable clothes so Weezie won't suspect anything if I turn up with mostly all new ones. Jesus, Bud, it's a quick jaunt to the eastern shore. You can chopper me in right from Langley. I've put down there before. There's plenty of level lawn between my house and the water."

"Hap, you do think of everything."

"Don't forget that I had good training in spycraft but spotting bureaucratic bullshit is something I figured out all on my own."

In the businesses Hap had purchased and then turned around, most demanded remedial attention and swift, decisive action. He had always started by first dismantling and then flattening the organization chart to improve efficiency. Nimble decision making followed by immediate implementation of bold action was always better when handled by a few rather than too many.

One thing that had hastened Hap's retirement from both his day job and side work for Langley was the bullshit. Like most burgeoning government agencies, the CIA had become a multiheaded and multilegged creature that seemed to him a bureaucracy on steroids with too many jockeying for a fast track to one of the seats of power in a corner office on the seventh floor. Such a convoluted and top-heavy structure also served to diminish if not curb individual initiative. Though Hap had signed on once more, being off book meant he would be reporting directly to one of those corner offices and in this case one occupied by Bud, who was one of the very few at Langley he could rely on.

CROSSCURRENTS

THOUGH HIS SELF-IMPOSED SEMIRETIREMENT had been designed to provide new terrain for discovery, Hap often found himself drifting back to what he had always done instead of what he should have been doing all along. The stable where he had been forced to live was full of formerly long-dormant reminders of those things he should have enjoyed. Instead, he had spent that precious time saluting the flag and unwittingly risking the lives of those he loved.

Beyond the leftover paraphernalia from his kids' youth, Hap had contributed some of those relics too, including three sets of golf clubs he no longer had use for. Even the seventeen acres of mostly wooded property that protected his privacy had evolved and was unrecognizable. Long gone were the once well-worn bridle paths and hiking trails that had been reclaimed by nature and were overgrown with new vegetation. It was easy to get lost. The only distinguishable trails were those deer had chosen to get at his luscious landscaping when the brunch buffet in the woods dried up over the winter. He had given up trying to keep them at bay with fencing and repellants and had resigned himself to allowing them to perform their own version of selective annual pruning.

The dog had always kept his company when no one else would, which should have been a clear signal that loneliness would become a steady companion. For too long, Hap had lived in the shadows, where most of his best work was done, but it had been a lonely place to hide. It was not where he wanted to dwell indefinitely, but it was nonetheless a familiar and comfortable refuge. Nevertheless, he was anxious to find out why that was so, and he hoped that Weezie could help him find the answers if he was willing to let down his guard long enough.

Unwilling to wait for her invitation and well aware it would be the last visit until they were bound for Italy, he resorted to spontaneity. On impulse, hardly a foreign response for Hap, he decided to surprise Weezie by showing up unannounced at her doorstep with only a small overnight bag and his dog. Because Hap hadn't yet had time to replace any of the cars destroyed in the fire, he drove the pickup, which meant a long trip. The usual four-hour drive took even longer because he had to make a few extra stops so Bailey wouldn't pee or poop on the seat, but they arrived just before bedtime as planned. Looking entirely out of place parked in such a fashionable neighborhood, the pickup was the first thing that gave Hap away when Weezie looked through an upstairs window in disbelief. After bounding down the stairs and opening the door, she actually laughed at the sight of him.

"Sorry, Hap, this is a respectable bed and breakfast that requires a reservation and doesn't permit domesticated or wild animals, so neither of you is welcome here."

"What if there's an exceptional Chardonnay in my bag?"

"Well, that changes everything. Come right in."

"Why thank you, ma'am. I thought you'd never ask."

"What possessed you to drive that old truck?"

"Well, since it's been sitting in the barn and hadn't been driven in several months, I thought I'd do the practical thing by taking an aimless, long drive to charge the battery, and somehow we ended up here. Go figure."

"I can't imagine it was all that comfortable for the two of you in the front seat along with luggage and dog food."

"Though there's nothing extravagant like cruise control or navigation, it's got an AM/FM radio and heater, so what more could man's best friend possibly want when riding up front with his master?"

Once inside, Bailey explored the entire three-story brownstone before settling for a comfy corner in the den to sleep. Hap and Louise chose the living room to sip the wine and continue trading their customary, fully charged banter. While she disappeared into the kitchen to fix some appetizers, Hap surveyed the vast bookshelves in search of something to browse and settled on an illustrated anatomy textbook. When Louise reappeared carrying assorted antipasti, she noted that Hap was engrossed in the book.

"So Hap, what's so mesmerizing about my anatomy book?"

"I was reading about the tongue. Did you know that pound for pound, it's the strongest muscle in the body? I would've guessed it was something else."

"No doubt."

"So it's not at all surprising that when there's new territory to be explored, you send in the tongue first."

"I'm speechless at what you find fascinating in nearly everything."

"Just plain curiosity at work. From what I've read here, wouldn't it seem to make perfect sense using the tongue to soften up any resistance before sending in the heavy artillery?"

"As usual, Hap, it's hard to argue with your reasoning and logic, but let's move on to something else that might be less perverse, maybe religion or politics. First, let me offer a professional and final observation about the tongue. Being stuck in the mouth all the time, it's grown accustomed to warm, dark, and wet places."

"See, Weeze? I knew you'd have an opinion."

In lieu of Weezie, he was fond of calling her Weeze when alone; he insisted that a single-syllabled nickname was more efficient and endearing. Though at first, she had thought it sounded more like wheeze or the near-death gasping of someone with COPD, she had grown to like it. Nevertheless, sometimes when she was upset with Hap, she called him Harrison in retaliation.

After discussing the divisive presidential campaign underway along with other newsworthy items, they were soon out of topics. Beyond the obvious, Hap allowed nothing more as to what prompted his surprise visit, deciding he wasn't ready to admit needing her guidance when seeking a long-term cure for loneliness. At least that's what he called it while remaining unwilling to ever admit to anything more debilitating ... such as depression or desperation.

In some ways, they were both damaged goods in need of repair. Because it was Hap who had restored the spring in her step, Louise felt duty bound to perform some restoration work on him as well. She was no dummy and was much better than others at getting five when adding two plus two. Instinctively, she knew where the conversation should be headed, and she broached it when the opportunity presented itself.

"Hap, I can't imagine how you operate so well and at such a high level when totally compartmentalized."

"It's easy. Some of those compartments are where I hide stuff and are off limits to everyone but me."

"Maybe it's time you opened those closet doors to shed a little light inside so you can clean out some of that old baggage you're storing."

"I'm saving that for a rainy day."

"You know, Hap, much like the mighty Mississippi, your waters run deep and service a huge watershed, but there are some dangerous crosscurrents coming from the tributaries."

"That's what makes such a river mighty when reaching the delta."

"It's still a long journey fraught with surprise, danger, and at times ... loneliness."

"Hey, Weeze, are you sure I'm worth saving?"

"You wouldn't be here and I wouldn't have let you in if I weren't sure of that."

"Then consider the permission granted to begin retooling my noggin so it will be all fixed up before we go to Italy."

"Gosh, Hap, I don't know where to begin."

"Try working backward from the happy ending."

"Okay, but you asked for it."

"Don't I always?"

"Try being serious. This isn't gonna work if you don't participate. Healing you isn't something I can do alone. You have to want it too."

"I always want it, Weeze. You should know that by now."

"That's a different problem, but let's get back to the main event. For starters, though you're probably capable of self-destruction, I don't think that's the ending you really want."

"Now *that's* scary stuff but maybe not terribly helpful, so how about just a short, preliminary diagnosis?"

"Oh Hap, it's so like you to be chasing immediate gratification without a hint of long-term commitment or satisfaction. Your problem is actually more attitudinal, and I have nothing in my tool kit to fix that on the fly."

"But it probably won't keep you from trying, right? You shrinks take much too long trying to fix what might not be broken. What I prefer is a battle-tested surgeon to perform a quick and improvisational field surgery without painkillers and be done with it."

"Look, Hap, all you need is just a little fine-tooling."

"That goes for you too, Weezie, and I'm at your service to get the job done right. In fact, how about right now?"

"See what I mean about instant gratification? You'd think I'd know by now never to expect a paucity of inappropriate libidinous responses from you."

"So I get points for at least being consistent?"

"No, but you do get to spend the night with me."

"That's a relief. I'd hate to do the hokey pokey and then turn myself around for a return trip home in the dark."

"Do the hokey pokey and call it a day, huh? So that's what it's all about?"

"Oh damn."

"What? Tongue-tied again, Mr. Franklin?"

"No. I forgot to pack my pajamas."

"You won't need any where you'll be sleeping."

"Then you can be sure I'll be overstaying my welcome. That is if you'll have me."

"Oh you bet I'm gonna have you."

PART II:
Ariosi

REPORTING FOR DUTY

THE SMALL JET THAT AWAITED HIM at the remote, private aviation terminal at Pittsburgh International bore no outward markings, and Hap was its only passenger. Clearance for takeoff must have been immediate as it was wheels up moments after he was aboard. There had been no chatter from the pilots beyond a summary greeting and verification of his identity. Only 190 miles as the crow flies, the flight took all of forty minutes. Though unnecessary, they were quickly vectored in for an immediate arrival slot ahead of commercial airline traffic awaiting instructions.

Upon deplaning, Hap recognized the black Suburban that would ferry him from the tarmac at Reagan National to Langley. Though it was the bottom-rung mode of standard transportation used by the CIA instead of the limo he'd been hoping for, it beat driving the Ford pickup, the only vehicle remaining of his former fleet.

He hadn't been to Langley in three years, so he was not surprised that the protocol for gaining entry to the innermost sanctum had been updated. Verification of identity before admission to the seventh floor went far beyond simple facial recognition and possession of the right credentials. The new procedure began with optical scanning and ended with his being swabbed for any trace of things that shouldn't be there. As always, once all the hurdles were overcome, he was escorted to Bud's office by an armed guard who gave Hap what seemed to be a sincere greeting.

"So you're the legendary Hap Franklin? It's a privilege to meet you, Mr. Franklin."

"Call me Hap. It's the nickname my momma gave me, and I'm sure legendary would be a stretch."

Hap considered it always important to guard against complacency even with those on the home team because they were the ones who enjoyed burnishing and elevating his image to a near action-hero level. Even without the notoriety and abundant hype that followed such an acclaimed agent, Hap had always sought to assure folks there that he was just another guy doing his job. Unfortunately, modesty was often something Hap could never get quite right, and knowing that, he had to work hard at it. But that time, he'd succeeded with his opening remarks and then did his best to be amusing by further engaging the guard.

"I remember where the DOD's office is, you know, and I don't really need an armed private docent to show me the way."

"You know the drill here, Mr. Franklin. You'd get the same treatment even if you were still one of ours."

"I suppose in some ways I'll always be one of yours."

The guard waited in the anteroom while Hap gave Bud's long-time secretary a quick smooch. A shapely strawberry blonde, her given name was Patti, but she was known by everyone as Sunny due to her disposition and perpetual tan. Though it was visible only from the neck up, Hap was certain that the rest of her cheerleader-like body was covered with the same sun freckles. In fact, sometimes, he hadn't been able to resist speculating about what it all looked like. What he didn't know was that Sunny shared the same private notion and would have eagerly taken it to the next level.

"Oh Hap, what a surprising refreshment you are, and what a tasty treat to have you back. I gotta confess that you're what's been missing in my life for too long."

"But Sunny, you haven't been missing in mine. In fact, I think of you every night before pulling up the covers."

"I bet! Now is this a social call, or are we fitting you for a new cape today?"

"Only if it comes with a scary mask and you take the measurements personally."

Their playful banter ended abruptly when Bud's voice echoed from within. "Okay, Hap, quit hitting on Sunny and get your sorry ass in here."

"Aye aye, Captain Hook."

As Hap had expected, Bud's office was a complete mess. Well-worn files and a mountain of fresh memoranda were strewn about—some arranged neatly in piles on the floor and others scattered in complete disarray atop his desk and conference table. An avalanche of paper waiting to cascade around him—That was the way Bud had always worked, and so far, it seemed to have worked for him. Even in a world dominated by electronic communication, Bud was old school and much preferred putting his hands on information when trying to make sense of it. He looked terrible, and based on the number of empty coffee cups and full ashtrays, Hap assumed that Bud had not had much sleep. Without rising to extend a proper greeting, Bud began as usual by bitching about all the wrong stuff.

"Christ, Hap! Do you have any idea how much your travel arrangements are gonna cost the American taxpayers today?"

"Not as much as every junior congressman's unnecessary boondoggle junket to God knows where. And Bud, don't ever forget how many hundreds of millions we confiscated from Cherkov when taking him down the last time, so I think I'm owed the occasional perk."

"Because you're off book, I had to borrow a fuckin' plane from the air force to fetch you here."

"We both know a shitload of the CIA's budget is hidden from sight in the armed forces, so I'm not sure that matters. What *really* matters is to be *where* it matters *when* it matters. Well here I am, so try to fake being happy to see me."

"Indignant as always, but I hardly expected a heightened level of compunction from you. I imagine you've never been appropriately deferential when in the presence of your superiors."

"Beyond our Savior, I'm not sure I have any superiors. Born in August, I'm a true Leo, and you should know a lion never loses sleep over the opinions of sheep."

"Maybe you were just born under a bad sign, Hap."

"Look, Bud, you know I flunked obedience school, don't roll over or heel well, and have never been good at repentance, so let's just get down to business."

"Damn. No more foreplay?"

"You're not my type, but you'll be spellbound by what I have to tell you."

Hap told Bud about receiving the emailed threat from Cherkov just before his cell phone was permanently disabled.

"So you got hacked. So what?"

"No, Bud, you don't get it. My electronic technology and identity are probably better guarded than the CIA's. I had a top PhD at MIT layer me up with the latest cybersecurity protocols for just this kind of thing. He assured me I'd be completely off the grid."

"It wouldn't be the first time an underpaid university scientist from our side had been compromised by the Russkies."

"No, Bud, it's bigger than that. I'm betting Cherkov is playing a new game now. Forget the arms dealing and dirty bombs. We have more to fear from him if he's developing sophisticated malware on a big scale."

"That's only a hunch."

"Look, you probably already know I've been running a little hedge fund since retiring from the big leagues. I'll let you in on a secret. The term hedge fund is a misnomer. They're really hunch funds, and the successful hunches at Sterling Capital were all mine."

"Everyone knows you unscrupulous Wall Street bastards are overpaid, but I never knew it was no more than a guessing game."

"Not quite, Bud. In fact, it's not too terribly different from what you do here—gather, analyze, verify, and then act decisively on good intel. That said, I gotta confess we made big commitments or as you might call them, bets, and sometimes more on instinct than intelligence, but I'd never admit that under oath. Let's just say I'm blessed with either outstanding investment acumen or blind luck. Take your pick."

"Not to diminish the reason you're here, but tell me why you're still rolling those loaded dice."

"It was hard leaving the game behind. I just couldn't go cold turkey."

"Maybe you missed the limelight too, having gone from *Who's Who* to something like *Who's That?*"

"Not really, Bud, and besides, though it's a far cry from the tens of billions Sterling Capital managed for institutional clients, it's not chump change. Making big bets keeps me engaged and on top of my game, so it's really for my amusement, though I do have a few outside investors. It's a very informal thing and unregistered, so I can dabble in listed securities and take private equity positions. Not bound by any needless regulations, there's no unnecessary paperwork. Think of it as an unfettered and freewheeling greedy pursuit of dazzling returns, but mostly just for grins."

"So what are the potential returns from these little hunches of yours?"

"Can't predict the future, Bud, but past results have been good. Lady Luck keeps blowing the right stuff on my dice, and the returns have never been less than thirty percent."

"Per year? Jesus, Joseph, and Mary, Hap. So why haven't you invited me into your little circle of prosperity?"

"C'mon, Bud, I don't mean to be presumptuous or condescending, but the price of admission is probably a tad beyond your reach. Besides, I don't even issue any reports beyond a single-page handout at our annual lunch."

"Like how much for starters?"

"It's ten million to play. Look, if things go sideways for a while or the fund loses some serious dough, we can't have a skittish investor aboard who's betting more than his lunch money let alone the entire farm. I have just a handful of investors, all close friends who've known me for years, and none of them is interested in cashing out and paying capital gains."

"Fine. I'll just stumble along with my little chickenshit savings in a mutual fund."

"Good idea just so it's a no-load index fund."

"Okay, Hap, once again, you got my attention, so let's finish this up before the world comes to its knees."

"Bud, this thing with Cherkov is serious shit, much more important than simply making big bucks on a gamble. If I'm right, besides the upcoming election, our national defense and power grid could be compromised, and that would mean the entire economy would falter. Hell, life as we know it is at stake."

Speculation was the agency's specialty, and unlike so many other theories that landed in Bud's lap, this one seemed credible. Given the CIA's private skepticism about the administration's ability to solve such a problem, he also knew that covert action was required when diplomacy was impossible. As was his custom, after a long incredulous look, Bud finally agreed not only to devote ample internal resources but also to cast a wider net to include other agencies that might shed some light on Hap's hunch.

Once Hap left, Bud buried his head in his hands, which was the way he worried and strategized. Always the skeptic, he had to play it all out in his mind before taking a decided stand on mustering the troops he had just promised to deliver. Given all

42 | *STRANGERS NO MORE*

Hap had done and sacrificed for America, his hunch could not be ignored, and though he had never once been wrong since joining the ranks, this was one of those times that Bud prayed he would be.

LIVING THE DREAM

EVERYONE KNEW THAT HAP HAD IT MADE except for Hap, who wasn't at all sure he had made it. Though never encouraging speculation about his wealth, neither had he refuted the claims made by others. As a result, he remained an anomaly in a tony place like Fox Chapel. What his friends and neighbors found difficult to do was to reconcile the guy who once climbed into limousines with the one whom they'd seen jumping on his garden tractor.

Hap's propensity for thrift was proverbial among all who knew him well. Courtesy of the strongly embedded if not inescapable DNA of his paternal Pennsylvania Dutch ancestors, his parsimony came to him naturally. He was a ninth-generation Pennsylvanian from a long line of enterprising Swiss-German farmers who had appreciated the value of everything and wasted nothing. They had been doing so since their arrival in 1694 from the Aare River Valley north of Bern, Switzerland. When they departed the lands of the Habsburg monarchy, the vast Holy Roman Empire included a mix of languages and ethnicities under the reign of Leopold I. The German-speaking areas that later became Germany, Austria, and Switzerland included abundant culture, but that was concentrated mostly in large cities including Vienna, so there was little more than hard work for Hap's ancestors to engage in.

Accomplished if not prominent dairy farmers and herders, they simply continued the same hard life after arriving in what would become Pennsylvania because it was all they knew. It was no wonder they settled in another rich and fertile valley, the Cumberland Valley, where most of their offspring remained. What drew them to the New World and land of opportunity was hard to pinpoint more than three hundred years later. Was it to escape religious persecution or their hardscrabble existence? If so, they had succeeded only in trading in one life for another that was all too similar. What they brought to the emerging colonies were callouses hardened by honest labor along with the redeeming qualities of determination, conviction, persistence, and abiding faith.

There was another reason his ancestors had left western Europe that was both logical and foresighted. Apparently, they had been astute enough to recognize the economic reality of a future without sufficient land. Over a long time, any parcel of land no matter its size could not sustain an ever-growing family. A growing number of descendants put a great demand on finite parcels of land and the limited bounty they produced.

After learning of the British colonization of vast lands known as the Americas and before abundance turned to scarcity, those who were among the most enterprising set sail in search of unlimited acreage and greater if not greener pastures.

Except for summers Hap spent on his uncle's farm in his youth, the only other farm Hap had ever visited belonged to the CIA, and the lessons he had learned there were from a horse of a different color. His father had been the first to abandon that stoic life by moving to the big city after college, but despite his new city-slicker status, he never managed to shake off the old virtues. Therefore, it was not surprising or unexpected that Hap felt duty bound to pay his allegiance to those who had preceded him. His homage was never given begrudgingly but rather with pride.

There was a second intrinsic dimension to Hap, one that was often at odds with his father's heritage. His mother was learned and sophisticated, and she had excelled in the arts, most notably music. A popular singer with her own weekly radio show, she entertained a grateful national audience of fans prior to the advent of television and her marriage. As her firstborn, Hap largely put an end to her career.

As opposed to his father's humble and modest background, Hap's mother's history was far different. Her earliest traceable ancestor was Guy de Balliol, who had accompanied William the Conqueror to England during the Norman Conquest in 1066. Two centuries later, his descendant, John de Balliol, became king of the Scots in 1292 and was the progenitor of the Clan MacGregor lineage that emerged in the early fourteenth century, about the same time the Black Death arrived in Scotland.

The plague lasted nearly a hundred years and killed a third of the population, but his mother's thinning bloodline continued throughout Great Britain until washing ashore in the New World. Though lacking a crown or requisite purse to confirm her royal pedigree, she had a rich and noble character, a much better substitute. Her refined influences on Hap were equally pronounced and embraced no matter the often-competing instincts he had inherited from his father. Notwithstanding the long running competition between those ancestral influencers, Hap had come to believe that simple hex signs always dominated heraldic coats of arms.

Oddly enough, Hap's DNA strands were in conflict with each other when it came to engaging in armed conflict on the battlefield or taking another's life. Curiously, his mother's four-times great-grandfather was a decorated colonial patriot who had rejected King George's tyranny and fought hard to establish the new nation. Though only one was needed, Hap's Sons of the American Revolution application included seven other ancestors who had served in the Revolutionary War, one directly under General Washington. Though they were fiercely opinionated, the ancestors on Hap's father's side had been for the most part pacifists, and when hearing the distant cannon fire from Gettysburg during the Civil War, they had simply kept tilling the soil, tending their crops, and milking their herds twice a day to feed the Union Army.

Because both parents were so strong willed, it wasn't surprising that their four children had struggled to define their own paths while being pulled in different directions. Their gene pool was an odd soup but nevertheless nourishing. Hap had never been confused by the dichotomy; instead, he had embraced the best elements each parent had contributed to the mix. However, he had not been naïve enough to imagine he could escape the lingering ancestral residue that guided his thoughts and behavior.

Though he wanted for nothing, Hap rarely overpaid for anything. He always bought the best and took damn good care of things, expecting them to last forever. When Brooks Brothers turned overseas to source affordable clothing for the masses, Hap began having bespoke suits made by London tailors. The same could be said for most footwear. When seventy percent of shoes were being manufactured in China, he resorted to bench-made shoes from England and from the few struggling domestic cobblers who remained in New England.

Some thought his regal appearance was intentional, but to Hap, it was never about preening like a peacock. He had had his fill of strutting long ago when he was the drum major of his high school marching band. Rather, it was all about buying goods of only the highest quality and rewarding those who made them with his patronage. Besides, it wasn't his fault that good stuff wasn't homemade any longer. America had outsourced virtually everything and had ended up awash in cheap imports. Engineered for obsolescence, once such tawdry things broke or wore out, they were nearly impossible to repair and usually cheaper to replace. Unlike Hap, not nearly enough consumers were fed up, so the cycle continued unabated as employment became America's chief export.

His retirement should have been a time for thanksgiving and rejoicing, but it wasn't. Hap found it harder than he had imagined to disconnect from one life and plug into another. Hanging up his spurs had never been something he had looked forward to. When the time arrived, despite having amassed a fortune and all the toys he could ever play with, he was emotionally unprepared to go it alone, especially after Kate's death. She was irreplaceable as the steadying influence in balancing Hap's perpetual high-wire act while serving two masters—Sterling Capital Management and the CIA. Even then, his allegiance was conflicted by knowing both were the wrong overlords, but that hadn't prevented him from obligingly saluting them.

Though often deriding his old-fashioned views and methods, Kate was amused by and even silently championed the tactics he used when defending them. On some level, Hap was sure Kate had admired what she routinely called his Byzantine thinking. Sure, it was complicated and depended on close examination of granular details before rendering a decision, but that was a part of him that had attracted her from the get-go. Knowing that Hap's reasoning was sound and that once he made a decision, he rarely backed off, Kate usually let him have his way. When the kids were bold enough to chime in, she reminded them that such efforts would be in vain because their father had already made up his mind and would end up doing what he wanted anyway.

He had only himself to blame for abandoning his day job at Sterling and occasional side work for the country long before he would have been obliged to do so. The flip side was that he ended up with far more time than any of his contemporaries had to do whatever he wanted. What few suspected was that Hap's bucket list was exceptionally long. He knew there was only so much more he could do with the time remaining on his clock. Unlike the typical retiree, he had nothing on his punch list including leisure activities. Instead, as before, he was devoted to only those tasks, challenges, and chores that involved exhaustive labor—either physical or mental.

As Kierkegaard had observed, much of life could be understood only backward but it had to be lived forward. His inability to fully comprehend what his past had wrought often bedeviled Hap's agenda for the future. Having reached the pantheon of his trade, maybe he had already lived the dream and needed to reconcile himself to that before moving forward. But not considering it a pressing dilemma, he failed to see much value in devoting any more time to pondering such a notion. Besides, something like that probably wasn't solvable anyway even with the help and patience of a good shrink.

HIDING THE LIE

H AP HAD BEEN HIDING THINGS FOR A LONG TIME. The list even included his full name, which he had covered up beginning in grade school. Though perhaps his parents were well intentioned, by naming their firstborn Benjamin Harrison Franklin, they had unwittingly saddled him with an unwelcome burden. Knowing early on that it would be difficult getting through life as Ben Franklin, he began using B. Harrison Franklin instead, but even his middle name didn't work. Harrison sounded haughty, and because it was a real mouthful for other kids, he adopted Hap, the nickname his parents had always used at home, as a permanent handle. Privately, he always thought of himself as Benjamin Harrison Franklin, and he liked the sound of it, but he rarely spoke it out loud. Concealing his legal identity at such an early age probably marked the beginning of a life lived in shadows, so it was no wonder that hiding beneath a cloak of anonymity became second nature for him down the road.

With Kate gone, the intricate mosaic that had been his life appeared shattered beyond recognition, and he accepted that reassembling the puzzle would be a challenge. Gone was the precision with which he once had executed every action, or so he feared. This time felt like being strapped to a roller-coaster that slowed to a crawl near the top when most riders were afraid it might slide back down and hurtle to the ground before reaching the peak. Either way, Hap couldn't stand being aboard anything that could falter, especially with anyone else but himself at the helm. He had always had control issues, but that was another distinguishing characteristic of a good spy.

He knew Kate had long suspected what his side work was all about, but she had had the good sense never to ask or confront him about it. If she had, he might have read her in on some of it but never the dangerous elements. Kate had had enough to worry about without his sharing his fears. Besides, she would never have understood why he did what he did. If she worried, and he was certain she had, it didn't show. Maybe she was afraid to acknowledge his other dimension for fear it would smother the man she had married. Life was like that—What you didn't know couldn't hurt you—But for Kate, that wasn't true. She died because of what he did in the shadows, so it was his fault.

Apart from Kate, no one else ever had a clue about Hap's dark side, which was the way he wanted it. Nevertheless, the hard years he spent wearing the mask of deception had taken their toll. All he wanted was to be left alone while pursuing some possible happiness with Weezie.

At Camp Peary, Hap had been trained to do things he could never talk about. For starters, the curriculum at the Farm brought a whole new meaning to the concept of the pass/fail courses offered at conventional places of higher learning. Passing meant you stayed alive but possibly only long enough to fail the next time. It wasn't much different from the anticipation before that roller-coaster ride—knowing that sooner or later your number was up but hoping it wasn't this time.

There wasn't much distinction between a covert operative and an accomplished assassin except that using the latter tag was strictly forbidden by the brass at Langley. They would never admit publicly or privately to being in the discretionary killing business, but that's what it often was. Looking back on it with seasoned perspective, Hap realized that every time he went to the Farm, he left a piece of himself behind. Still, as Bud had recently said, Hap was "once the best they had, and maybe still was." Although for years he had told lies for a living, Hap wasn't about to deceive himself with such a notion. He knew the worst lies were the ones you told yourself.

The duplicity had become harder to manage, and perhaps the burden of guilt over Kate had reached the level of being potentially self-destructive. He couldn't allow that to happen, and he vowed to think about it no more until the current crisis with Cherkov passed. Bud was probably right—There weren't many like Hap, and this time, his skill set was desperately in demand. Nevertheless, he worried that he might never again be good enough to win all the time, but the specter of failing this time was absolutely unacceptable.

LAMENT

HIS HAD BEEN A NEAR PERFECT LIFE that he had painstakingly constructed along the way. Even the mismatched pieces were thoughtfully put together to make it all work ... until Kate was removed from the puzzle. When she died in the fiery crash, Hap knew it was no accident as too many things didn't add up. Trusting his instincts, he began a relentless pursuit of the truth, and only after years of dogged determination and investigation following her suspicious death did he discover it. Once uncovered, he dispatched his own brand of justice. Taking it well beyond an eye for an eye, Hap made sure at least one of the culprits had paid dearly with his own life in a grim and grisly fashion.

Until then, all his targeted eliminations had been clean and without having caused needless suffering, but Hap made up for a lifetime of merciful killings with the wretch who had betrayed him by sacrificing Kate. The fact that he was an American and also in service to the flag made no difference. Hap had always considered rules to be guidelines, so it hadn't been hard to break the cardinal one that began with thou shalt not ... especially in the name of just retribution. In a roundabout way, Hap had come prewired for the job. Seeking and taking revenge was the easy part. Living with the guilt thereafter had proven harder though not unbearable.

When his outright grieving for Kate was over, Hap found he could tolerate the loneliness but couldn't outrun the sadness or shed the sorrow. Try as he might, he could not bring her back to life. Even the clear pictures of her that were once permanently lodged in his mind's eye were beginning to fade along with the memories they had evoked. He obsessed over the things he would miss without her by his side. Hap had always refuted the proverb of what the eye doesn't see, the heart doesn't grieve over, but he was reluctantly becoming a believer in that maxim. Though he had never been the kind who looked backward to relive trials or relish triumphs, with a future as uncertain as his, Hap struggled when pondering what the next chapter might look like. Stress was accelerating the aging process—he could see it in the mirror, and passing into physical decrepitude wasn't something he would permit.

Somewhere, he had lost his way and couldn't find the path back. Even his home's garden and grounds, places where Hap had always been able to find emotional serenity and a private refuge from the daily grind, no longer held his interest. Sloth, whether intellectual or manual, had always been anathema to Hap, and he recognized its danger of pushing one along to the precipice. It was nearly impossible for him to carry on with the knowledge that he had a much larger score to settle, and the dilemma was of the sort he had never before faced. He could languish in sorrow or hatch a plan to go after the one who had ordered Kate's death.

All Hap had discovered was that the reason for Kate's murder was nothing more than an outrageously bad move by the Russians in a serious and prolonged tit for tat game played with the United States. A few years earlier, one of the black-bag jobs that had fallen into Hap's lap had been to whack a Russian double agent, and if all had gone according to plan, that would have been the end of it. But it hadn't, and it wasn't.

Hap had been in charge of the team carrying out the hit, but he technically hadn't been the shooter. The job was botched when his triggerman missed the second kill shot to the head that ended up hitting the Russian spy's wife instead. The first shot had been clean, and the target was lights out before hitting the ground, but a second errant shot had paralyzed his wife. The bad side of memory was that it wasn't erasable, and that assignment was one Hap's mind would never be able to unsee or undo. With a little mandatory psychiatric intervention from CIA shrinks, Hap eventually got over the grief but not his role in the loss suffered by an innocent bystander. Langley's euphemism for it was collateral damage; it was just business. But killing Kate in retaliation was a blatant violation of the rules. Hap was done with sanctimony and wanted his own rightful revenge.

Though the American who, like Judas Iscariot, had betrayed Hap's identity for a mere handful of silver, Kate's actual assassination likely had been carried out by Federal Security Service (FSB) agents at the behest of the Russian president or czar as he was dubbed by Langley. Nothing so overt could have occurred without direct orders from or a blessing by the czar. Taking down one of his own had become routine for him, but murdering a foreigner was an audacious act and fraught with perilous diplomatic consequences for the motherland. The Kremlin had been down that road before but never with an American target.

What the czar might not have known was that Hap had arranged for a private courier to deliver an anonymous and heartfelt letter of apology along with a princely sum of rubles to the Russian agent's widow. He had done such things before quietly and without fanfare in the name of charity but never when prodded by guilt and remorse. If the Kremlin had been aware of his compassion, perhaps Kate's life would have been spared. But unlike Hap, who was haunted by the memories of all those whose lives he had extinguished, the body count for the czar was far too high, and he didn't seem the type who grieved over anything.

It was well known that Russian dissidents were routinely silenced by poisoning and when necessary occasionally on foreign soil, where avoiding political blowback was more of a problem. A strong denial by the Kremlin would be issued and never walked back, and that was that. The czar would put on his public mask of synthetic indignation when such things happened only to privately congratulate the killers thereafter. If their identities ever became known, they met the same fate as those they had silenced. The czar's far-flung apparatus of oppression operated without boundaries. But taking down a CIA operative's wife was outside the box, and something so provocative couldn't easily be asserted by Team USA in a diplomatic way.

Hap knew from the start that even this most egregious of transgressions would never be avenged. Getting to the czar was unthinkable and preposterous, but that didn't stop him from thinking about how it might be accomplished. Hap had always been drawn to a challenge, especially when the odds were stacked against him, but he realized that this one would have to wait for another time. To save himself, he had to resist the temptation to right the wrong, which could consume him. Reluctantly, he would live with the lament and maybe someday find a way to get even.

So after two years with only his dog, Bailey, for company, Hap had decided it was time to move on, but as was his custom, he did so in an unusual way. Was it really folly to go back in time and try to fix what had been broken to create a new future? Even if it were, Louise was one of the best places to start. The stakes were high, and if it failed, it failed. But an outcome of all or nothing was preferable to never taking the initiative and pining away alone. In short order, he had done just that, and it was how Hap and Louise eventually rediscovered a past that had brought them to a present that was fast becoming a promising future.

THE BACKSTORY

IT WAS A GOOD THING WEEZIE HAD NOT WITNESSED the explosion of Hap's home. She had no stomach for confrontation, especially when it spiraled out of control and in this case more resembled outright warfare. She had always been like that even when they had first met in junior high. When tensions rose among their classmates, she was the one who would smooth things over before they erupted into conflict. That calming ability no doubt accounted for why she had become so accomplished in the field of stress disorders. Attracting millions in annual grants, the celebrated Louise Porter, MD, had become a significant one-woman profit center for Johns Hopkins Hospital. Her endowed chair as a tenured professor at the university's medical school was just one of the many ways its administration tried to maintain her loyalty.

She was a big deal and could easily write her own ticket to anywhere in the world, but from the start, Hopkins felt like home to her. In spite of her rock star status in medical circles, Louise was also known as just plain Weezie to her inner circle of friends, and Hap had become the closest over the last few years.

Though absent from most of his life, Weezie had lived on in Hap's imagination and played a vital role. So it was not surprising that once reunited after decades of being apart, they presented as friends in need who quickly became friends indeed. The trouble with temptations was that they had short shelf lives and lasted only so long before becoming obsessions. So smitten with her had Hap been back in seventh grade that his adolescent longing had become a lifelong obsession, and he hungered for her still.

It was no different for Louise. In the beginning, it had all happened so innocently and gradually that she didn't realize how involved she was becoming until it was too late. Though her infatuation with Hap had started as a teenager, she had no idea how fulfilling but dangerous such a lifelong liaison would be. Inexorably drawn to each other for reasons real and imagined, they were star-crossed from the very start. There had been occasions over the years when it could have happened, but it just hadn't.

First had been the awkwardness of adolescence, and that was followed by separation during college and finally the busyness and distraction of what life was serving up during their early adulthood. Sometimes she blamed Hap but other times herself for missing those chances. So when the right circumstance came along the last time, she was ready to embrace it with the certainty that only decades of hindsight could provide. One thing was certain—For too many years, it had been only about what could have been but wasn't, and she was determined to fix that.

Oddly enough, they had been thrust together to plan their high school reunion. Though innocent enough at the start, their working together for a year even from afar soon reignited the simmering, long-lingering passion from their past. Revealing themselves to each other was an intimate experience in itself. In ways resembling a slow striptease, it was like peeling an onion one layer at a time. Sharing their joys, trading their triumphs, admitting their regrets, acknowledging their transgressions, and even confessing their sins became their routine. One by one, they even managed to dispel all the mistaken impressions and falsehoods each had harbored about the other from their long distant past. Eventually, there were no more secrets between them … except one, and that was his clandestine side work to keep the country safe from outside harm.

Their reacquaintance came at the right juncture for Hap, who needed to stop wrestling with the bitterness of Kate's death. The timing was also good for Louise as she too was vulnerable, particularly while trying to figure out an escape plan from a loveless third marriage to an absentee husband. The reunion became the seminal event that allowed them to reconnect the dots from their past and start getting on with completing the journey. After an extended courtship from a safe distance—she in Baltimore and he in Pittsburgh—their intimacy eventually prevailed as they had known it would. Once rekindled, their fervid love became boundless and was the kind of epic adventure found only in the very best books.

Louise loved her work, and before Hap came along, the only others she ever had time for were her two daughters, who would always be at the center of her being. She had been an adoring mother before and after her divorce from the girls' father, her second husband. Her work kept her busier than most docs, but eventually, loneliness gained traction and took over. She missed having someone, anyone, around to share the adventures of what life coughed up daily. After a decade of such solitude but long before getting entangled with Hap, she had made the mistake of marrying again—a third time to a Dmitri Cherkov, a Russian national. Almost from the beginning, she knew it wasn't going to work out, but she couldn't begin to fathom what a problem Dmitri would become—for herself and in time Hap as well.

What she hadn't known about her new husband could have filled an oversized binder. Langley of course had such a file. A global arms dealer, he had been on the radars of most civilized countries' intelligence services for years. A Russian oligarch and former KGB colonel, he was a known longtime crony of the Russian president. This liaison made it possible for Cherkov to pilfer Russia's stockpile of obsolete Soviet-era weaponry and sell it to the highest bidders, which were usually unstable regimes and renegade jihadists in the forever shifting sands of the Middle East. Lately, it was suspected that the munitions Cherkov sold were more sophisticated, including chemical and biological weapons.

Marrying Louise had provided Cherkov both social cachet and US residency though he was rarely at home; he had spent most of his time in Russia or aboard his yacht—one of the world's largest that could be sailed to any port in advance of his arrival. The luxurious vessel was stocked with the finest of everything, including young women who engaged their host in making sure his fondest fantasies came true and all unmet needs were satisfied. It was no secret that Cherkov really had no use for Louise after duping her into a marriage for his convenience only. For Louise, it was a conundrum she wasn't sure how to solve. Besides, while balancing her busy medical practice and role as a doting mother, she could not afford any more distractions or complications.

Spousal rejection was usually as traumatic as life got. Louise had been down that road and on the receiving end of that twice before. She hadn't known it then but had since learned from her work with patients that wives usually didn't see it coming until there was another woman in the picture, and once that was the case, it was all but over. Unlike penguins, wolves, and coyotes, too many folks were incapable of mating for life, and the escalating divorce rate proved it.

While trading up wouldn't always define the second wife, trading down in age was assured. Few men understood the pain of abandonment; they simply left their discarded baggage for someone else to deal with and ran for the emergency door. Some divorcées learned something from the experience while others did not.

This time, the tables were turned, and Louise's role would be different from what it had been the last two times. But upon discovering things about Dmitri she hadn't before and well aware of what he was capable of, Louise had feared taking the next step and decided to simply mark time. A determined woman, she was able to keep all the balls in the air … until Hap became yet another one to juggle.

Due to widespread surveillance of Cherkov, once a clandestine operative like Hap got mixed up with Louise, all the alarm bells and whistles went off at Langley. Sleeping with the enemy, or in this case the enemy's lawful wife, which was what Hap, a CIA agent, was doing was unprecedented, but at the same time, it presented Langley with an opportunity. Hap's and Louise's innocent affair had provided Bud and his colleagues at the CIA a convenient way in. But Cherkov had discovered his wife's infidelity first, and he couldn't risk losing her for cover. Though he cared not for Louise, Cherkov was nevertheless infuriated that he had been cuckolded. As any proud man would be, he was enraged and then consumed with concocting possible means of revenge.

Inasmuch as he tried to resist the temptation, Cherkov could not refrain from going after Hap for the transgression, which served only to presage his own downfall. All along but unbeknown to Louise, Hap had been involved in foiling the plot and capturing Cherkov. Playing their part in the deception, CIA spooks informed her of Cherkov's criminal activities and supposed demise. They also played a big role in securing a bona fide death certificate. Missing a body for proof, that proved to be a protracted legal process, but it eventually resulted in a death decree issued by a sympathetic judge. That permitted Louise to claim partial ownership of her supposedly late husband's confiscated assets. Of course those assets were far more significant than she had ever known because Langley released only some of the seized property after awarding much of it to their own coffers.

For Weezie, it was nothing short of an emancipation once the emotional burden was lifted. With Cherkov presumed dead and no longer a threat, the relationship between Louise and Hap flourished. With Louise now newly single, she was no longer forbidden fruit. For Hap, that didn't make her any less desirable but instead even more of a narcotic. He felt entitled to what were once misbegotten perks of their relationship, and his addiction to them only increased.

Unfortunately, what Bud had never told Hap and therefore what neither Hap nor Weezie knew was that Cherkov was alive; after an exhaustive interrogation, he had been traded away to the Russian president by higher powers.

A DOC IN DEMAND

DR. LOUISE PORTER WAS ACCORDED WORLDWIDE celebrity status in her field of behavior modification. Most of that was attributable to the growing scholarly body of work she contributed, and some was the hype carefully spun by her employer to keep her on top of the heap. Like any other field, medicine had become a cutthroat business, and its biggest players were expert in burnishing their reputations. Johns Hopkins worked hard to elevate its profile and those of its famous medical stars. For Louise, who shunned the spotlight, it meant having way too many speaking engagements orchestrated and mandated by the university or its primary cash cows—the teaching hospital and medical school. At first, she had resisted the drumbeat set by the folks in public relations, but she had eventually come to her senses and for the most part toed the line. As she once told Hap, "The beat goes on" and she could ill afford to "rock the boat."

Louise had hit her professional stride when PTSD was threatening to become the all-inclusive explanation for fear, trauma, and anxiety. Initially, it was Dr. Porter's reputation alone that drew standing room only crowds to her lectures. But the reason for her ongoing popularity was her ability to bring the science alive by example. It almost didn't matter if the case studies she used were real; the point was that they were fun and engaging for her spellbound audiences. Be they compulsive stockers, serial killers, white supremacists on a rampage, or drugged-up soldiers returning from some faraway desert battlefield, she could diagnose the underlying causes of their neuroses and explain away the dark sides of these flawed characters.

More than most, and as a lifetime observer from the sidelines, Hap had no trouble understanding her achievements. Not all of them had come easily, and that made them even more cherished. She had overcome much of what life had thrown at her. Relying on sheer spunk and determination, she enrolled in medical school much later than most and amid the pressures of an already hectic life of raising two children without much help.

Hap's early adolescent attraction to Louise had evolved into a lifetime fascination turned obsession. She made loving her an easy decision. Beyond her quick wit and overall brilliance, there were so many other enticing sides to Louise that Hap had discovered only during the most recent years. Empathetic with her patients and encouraging to her students, she showed genuine kindness and thoughtfulness to all who crossed her path. Another newly discovered indicator of compatibility was that she always brought an opportunistic approach to the bedroom, but she mostly stayed within the guardrails of acceptable behavior. Though reluctant to ever admit it, most men considered such an element a priority and necessary to seal the deal.

When not wearing her lab coat and heels, Louise preferred casual attire, which was the way Hap had always thought of her. When a teenager, he liked the way she looked when doing honest chores in and around the barn next to her family's country home in Fox Chapel. That usually meant she was clad in snug blue jeans, boots, and a rumpled work shirt—a look she could make sultry without even trying. Perhaps it also struck a familiar chord in the complicated strand of his Pennsylvania Dutch DNA. Louise also liked doing things other girls didn't including camping in the woods, canoeing, fishing, hunting, and routinely skinny-dipping after dark in their pond.

Like most veterans of World War II, Louise's father had insisted that all his children learn not to fear but instead to develop a healthy respect for firearms. He patiently trained them using both a .22 rifle and shotgun but never a handgun. His eldest daughter became the family's best marksman no matter if the target was stationary or moving. Living in the country provided lots of the latter type including varmints that posed a threat to her father's garden. It wasn't long before Louise could nail a groundhog on the run at fifty paces. Even then but especially currently, there weren't many women who came equipped with such expertise. Though she had never touched a gun since, because it was like riding a bicycle, her skills with firearms developed in youth remained intact and were recallable on demand. She hadn't deliberately avoided guns; she simply couldn't imagine being confronted with a situation that called for violating the do no harm part of the Hippocratic oath she had taken.

She was simply fun to be around despite being able to be so only on weekends. But the current arrangement worked well for both of them, and there didn't seem to be a pressing reason to change it. Weezie was a doc in demand while Hap was similarly pressed by a host of duties—some by design and others not as much so. Separation anxiety was something they never got used to, but they tolerated it during the weekdays. When Fridays arrived, the weekends were that much more satisfying and precious a time for recharging their batteries to deal with what they faced when apart.

RETROSPECTION

ALL HER LIFE, LOUISE THOUGHT OF HIM more than she should have and sometimes in ways she never should have, but Hap Franklin was hard to forget. Her daydreaming always began at the very beginning with the same fond recollection—a slow dance in seventh grade. It was the pivotal moment in a relationship that never happened. When he asked her to dance, she wasn't sure she should, but she desperately wanted to anyway. After all, he had a reputation for needing lots of attention, which wasn't something she was yet ready to give.

Taking her momentary hesitation as a yes, Hap had seized the opportunity by gently wrapping her in his arms. As she should have expected, he simply took control, and instead of resisting, she acquiesced. What followed surprised her. In a departure from his typical persona, he spoke softly and tenderly by whispering into her ear asking her all about herself. His questions were probing and provoking. She wondered if he had prepared them, had used them on other girls, or had been prompted by a genuine curiosity and interest in her alone. One thing was certain—Theirs was not the kind of first conversation teenagers typically had.

The encounter had stirred Louise inside and out. It had been a giddy sensation with feelings ranging from butterflies in her tummy to being overheated from head to toe. Even the memory of it still haunted her but in a good way. At her age then, the arousal she felt was not something she could yet understand. Exciting and full of wonder, the experience was over and above the kind of full-blown hot and sticky orgasms she would experience only years later. That night, Hap had moved her in an unfamiliar way, and the feeling was one she had never forgotten.

In its aftermath, Louise thought long and hard about Hap, but she was unable to reconcile the public and private versions. Perhaps he was just misunderstood by the others, who never got so much as a glimpse of his true side. To most onlookers, Hap seemed to be a candidate for one thing or another and on a continuous campaign trail to win at everything … and at all costs. Even then, he took chances and made big bets, which probably prepared him for the successes that followed. She had considered him overly driven to succeed, and she figured he'd either go places or burn out trying.

Her apprehensions about him were understandable, or so she tried to convince herself. Louise knew he was going to be more than a handful and hard to handle on a daily basis. He might even turn out to be the kind of boy her mother had warned her about. In the end, she decided that Hap was just too competitive and needy, and she was not up for that challenge. Plus, she had her pick of so many uncomplicated boys.

No one else ever knew how conflicted she was over Hap, and he remained the biggest secret of her youth for thirty years. Oddly enough, over those intervening years, it had been Weezie's mother who had often reminded her that Hap had been just the sort of guy she should have latched onto from the beginning. But realizing she had made the wrong decision even if for the right reasons, she didn't plan to make the same mistake again.

There had been a few opportunities over the years when they could have reconnected, but all were nothing more than mere touching points when their separate lives had briefly crossed. In hindsight and with the benefit of a scholarly perspective, Louise thought that she may have been trying to replace Hap all along with other equally strong-willed men. Unfortunately, they had all ended up hurting her. Hap may have too if they had followed a different path from the beginning, so it was probably best that they hadn't found each other until later in life. Maybe it was a blessing that it had happened the way it had. This time, it could be for keeps, and so far, the extended postponement of what they recognized as an abiding love had not diminished in its fervency. If it was true that once in a lifetime comes but once, she was determined to make sure Hap would be an exception.

Louise had come to grips with her past and finally realized that her marriages and most of her other relationships before Hap hadn't been failures but rather mistakes. She knew too that at their ages, they were well seasoned and reluctant to change their behavior. Despite her love for him, she was a different woman, not the type who could ever envision herself playing second fiddle on every score. Luckily, the game changer this time was that she was professionally equipped to deal with Hap's foibles and knew how to fix them.

PART III:
Adagio

PAYING THE PIPER

BECAUSE WEEZIE AND HAP HAD BEEN UNDER the assumption that Dmitri Cherkov had met his maker and perhaps under rather grim circumstances, life had gone on for them. In fact, they were having the time of their lives absent the specter of her former husband. Once released by the State Department under direct orders from the president, Chekov had a homecoming in Moscow, but it was no picnic. Even the CIA, which vigorously opposed freeing him, had gotten wind of his reception. Langley also suspected that Cherkov's release had been secured by the czar, to whom they already knew the American president was beholden.

The president and long-ruling tyrant of Russia, universally known as the czar by the free world's intelligence agencies, had finally had it with Dmitri Cherkov. Having grown weary of his onetime favorite oligarch's shenanigans and at times even skeptical of his absolute allegiance, the czar made sure that Cherkov was severely flogged within hours of landing at Sheremetyevo. The Federal Security Service, or FSB, had seen to that and maybe a little more for good measure. Once his wounds healed, Cherkov was publicly humiliated and ridiculed in front of key members of the Federal Assembly. Such a lesson was not lost on those who might have harbored thoughts of ever disobeying the czar. The private repudiation that followed was by the president himself, but without any witnesses.

Having risen to the rank of lieutenant colonel in the KGB, the long-reigning czar was well equipped for his position. Trained to be ruthless and a master of deception, he never betrayed anger publicly, but he was as calculating as any despot, and he always got even. Even his bland attempts to smile were plainly disingenuous. But he also knew better than most never to cut off any hand that could continue feeding his rapacity for riches. Besides, he would find it difficult to replace such a man in his inner circle. Smart, cunning, and resourceful, Cherkov was also loyal even if difficult to control, and he was among only a handful who understood and obeyed the oath of fealty.

Nevertheless, Comrade Cherkov's months-long disappearance while in CIA custody had proven costly for the czar. As with pirates at sea, others had soon captured the bounty and filled the void left by the collapse of the Cherkov empire. There was one big problem with that—The newcomers who were profiting from the spoils of Cherkov's illicit businesses were no longer paying the piper. The czar was further enraged because a substantial portion of Cherkov's assets had been seized by the Americans, a very personal and embarrassing affront. The Russian dictator considered the confiscated money his because he had been the one who had bestowed the favored status on Cherkov that had enabled the latter to prosper after paying the piper his due.

The Russian president's influence and extensive reach resembled a modern-day Attila the Hun but with a czar's imperial trappings. Much as he had been with the anointment of all his oligarchs, the czar had been choosy. The former Soviet Union was now no more than a kleptocracy for the few who governed. Men like Cherkov had been created to enrich the president in roundabout ways by plundering the resources of the motherland while impoverishing its people. The czar had learned the lesson of administering harsh financial punishment followed by a pardon from another de facto despotic ruler—the crown prince of Saudi Arabia, who had exacted billions of dollars from his own relatives based on nothing more than his whim.

It made no sense to kill or even cripple Cherkov for his foolish deeds as he could again be useful. Once rehabilitated by public censure and a torturous whipping, he could resume what he had been chosen for—replenishing the president's vast, secret coffers. His life was spared but not completely restored, as Cherkov's own fierce pride had been assaulted and forever damaged in a way that he could never forgive or forget. And though the indignities he had suffered had not been at the hands of Hap Franklin, they were certainly the result of having been bested by him.

METAMORPHOSIS

C HERKOV'S TRANSFORMATION BEGAN with surgery and a monthlong stay in the private clinic of a very gifted plastic surgeon in Geneva. His convalescence involved being enshrouded for two weeks when he could only peep through the mummifying dressing that surrounded his head. Finally, the medicated bandages came off, and with the addition of newly tinted contact lenses, he at last could assess the expensive result. When a mirror was placed in front of him, the anxious Cherkov only smiled. Though the face that returned his stare was nearly unrecognizable, he liked what he saw.

Part of the princely sum charged by the surgeon was meant to guarantee the patient's anonymity before and after the procedure. No one on the surgical team beyond the doctor ever saw more than a section of Cherkov's face at a time. Though the fresh veneer might provide a permanent camouflage, it would never conceal or fully erase his Russianness. His intentions were never that his new face be completely transformative by itself, but in tandem with other changes, that it would fool anyone who had ever known Dmitri Cherkov. However, though perhaps he was unrecognizable, there would forever remain one unmistakable telltale tag—his DNA, which could never be altered. The CIA had taken a sample of it when he had been in custody, so if need be, Cherkov could be identified if ever surfacing again as a threat to national security.

To ever get back on American soil, Cherkov's makeover needed to be complete. During recovery from the plastic surgery, he engaged a dialogue coach to replace his native accent with a nearly flawless American one. That part of the transition had taken nearly a year and had been harder than he had expected. American English had become a sloppy language that continued to evolve by borrowing from all others while turning its back on itself. Rules of grammar had atrophied and no longer governed either speech or the written word. To Cherkov, it was just another indication that Americans were getting lazy, fat, weak, and stupid. But he knew there was one who hadn't decayed, and he was the one whom he was after.

It took two years for Cherkov to fully recover his business and resume good standing with the Kremlin, and like a phoenix that had risen from the ashes, he had reemerged even more powerful than before. Much of the inspiration that fueled his meteoric rise was kept secret from all others. It had to be because it involved seeking his final revenge on the man he blamed for nearly ruining his life. It wasn't unusual for Cherkov to spend some of his executive time in quiet thought, though few suspected those thoughts were riveted solely on concocting a plan to destroy Hap Franklin—beginning with his home.

PARADISO

BEYOND RESTORING HIS TIMELY STREAM of payments, Cherkov had endeared himself to the czar in another way. Apart from resuming his previous business of dealing in arms, drugs, and other contraband including radioactive nuclear material, he diversified his activities to include pirating in cyberspace, which fascinated the Russian leader. Cherkov had even established a sophisticated and self-sufficient troll farm equipped with elaborate data-mining software that continued to vex and outfox the Americans. But beyond all manner of cybertheft, the czar was far more intrigued by Cherkov's abilities to wage ideological warfare with the West through a sustained disinformation campaign.

Employing only the best Russian, Asian, and Indian nationals as engineers, Cherkov set up shop in the Caribbean—a destination that proved to be especially tempting during the recruitment process. There, the unsuspecting techies would be transformed into the world's foremost cybercriminals. The gated and well-guarded compound was more like an all-inclusive Sandals resort as opposed to the prison it had been designed to be. The enchantment of the facility was itself sufficiently seductive to draw the most talented computer geeks. Even its name had been carefully chosen to convey the island's appeal; borrowing from Dante's *Divine Comedy*, Cherkov had named it Paradiso.

Complete secrecy and anonymity were the cardinal rules, and no outgoing contact with the outside world was permitted or for that matter even possible. After working long hours at their computer stations, the young trolls could enjoy all manner of recreation, sumptuous meals, and copious cocktails followed by casual, consensual sex. In fact, sport fucking was encouraged as it kept the horny drone bees happy and content. It was a paradise indeed for most of them, and so far, only a few of the hired hackers had resigned or requested a leave of absence to return to their home countries. To avoid arousing any suspicion among the others, all such requests were granted, but none of the trolls who had requested to leave ever made it off the island alive.

Woe be the girl who allowed herself to become pregnant. Paradiso's medical clinic could handle abortions, but it was neither equipped for nor had any interest in performing live-birth deliveries. That would distract the mothers and fathers from their real work, which was to target, exploit, and plunder unsuspicious victims and spread disinformation. Instead, the expectant parents would be offered a free trip to their homeland for an extended maternity leave. Such sabbaticals proved to be short-lived. Told they would be ferried to a nearby island with an airport, the naïve couple would eagerly board one of the Paradiso fleet's fishing boats—one specially equipped for the short journey. They would not even notice what was concealed beneath a tarp at the stern.

The camouflaged equipment was hardly high tech; it was a customized wood chipper that could turn an entire tree up to fourteen inches in diameter into mulch and sawdust. Not sadists like their employer, the sailors who manned the boat were merciful. While still alive, their passengers would be injected with a tranquilizer to escape the trauma of facing the chipper while conscious. After all, they were Russians, not barbarians. Besides, a limp body was far easier to carry and process than a resistant one was.

It was a quick and easy conversion. Life was over in a few pulverizing seconds. The lifeless bodies were fed through the jaws of death and jettisoned overboard in a scarlet plume of blood, sheared tissue, and shards of bone. The discharge chute spewed the carnage into the sea, where it became instant chum for the fish and eventually savory suppers for sharks. By intention, the boat would be turned into the wind to avoid any blowback of human debris. Cleanup would thereby be limited to hosing down the chipper with saltwater and a scented disinfectant. The crew might have nightmares, but it was part of their unofficial job description and an assignment for which they were handsomely compensated.

Cremation would have been a far simpler solution, but Cherkov himself had devised this macabre method of disposition. He was so fond of the procedure that he had insisted on witnessing the first execution. As expected, it fueled his perverse affinity for all manner of cruelty and torture. He was only fulfilled after casting a line into the stained pools of water once the big fish arrived for supper. He announced to the crew that whatever was hooked after taking the bait would become his meal that night. Though all aboard were sickened by the notion, one of them could not stomach it and puked overboard. Cherkov had shot him and then summarily fed him through the grinder for displaying such weakness.

Beyond possible discovery by other nations, Cherkov had wisely chosen Paradiso for another reason. Because it was not on Russian soil, the czar could not appropriate the compound. The czar was no fool and realized that this put him in the unfamiliar and awkward position of being indebted to one of his own oligarchs.

Once the fortress of electronic architecture was complete, Paradiso's cyber pirates could hack into virtually anything, which enabled rampant theft and other acts of criminality. Among the unsuspecting victims would be Hap Franklin. But the ultimate value of the enterprise to the czar was far simpler and a logical extension of Cherkov's new capabilities. Beyond the abundant riches that could be made, his overriding desire was to harness the outpost for sowing seeds of discord on American social media platforms. Of course, at the behest of the czar, Cherkov was only too happy to comply. In doing so, he made himself indispensable, and he once again resumed his rightful place as the czar's favored pawn.

LOWERING THE DRAWBRIDGE

T HE CZAR'S INTENTION AND LONG-RANGE GOAL was to upset the world order by first helping to elect a naïve and foolish imbecile as president of the United States and then watch Russia's ideological enemy slowly wither from the inside without any visible provocation from the outside. Encouraging death by suicide in this fashion would leave no perpetrator's fingerprints, so the real history of America's downfall could never be written.

Though the campaign rhetoric at election time had promised change, America's president forfeited his right to govern within hours of his inauguration. His first executive order had been a precursor of what would be an onslaught of changes, and most were bad ones. Disinformation, deceit, and downright lies were broadcast daily to the gullible citizenry that had put him in charge. For a while, even the media remained fairly restrained in factually challenging his politically contentious actions, pronouncements and scandalous behavior. Buffoonery and heresy at such a level was not something they were prepared to comprehend let alone report on.

What the enlightened majority feared most was the president's daily provision of kindling to stoke an uncontrollable wildfire the likes of which would prove devastating. Spurring divisiveness on every issue including racism was simple sport for the president, but it risked turning the American clock backward and its government into dysfunctional chaos.

Representing a new and distinctive flavor of danger to most, he empowered like-minded others who also found it unnecessary to separate public and private conduct no matter how reproachable. It seemed there was no escape from the irreparable damage visited on his dim-witted followers. His only legislative effort was to muscle the quick enactment of an intricate but familiar tapestry of subsidies and entitlements doled out to those who replenished his political war chest. The public outrage voiced by centrists and those left of center was tempered by total allegiance from the right. As a candidate, he had gained traction from both sides—the disadvantaged who harbored the same thoughts he espoused and the privileged whose primary concerns were limited to a falling stock market or an increase in taxes. Once in office, he was unafraid to vilify both ends of the congressional spectrum to keep them in line. With their obliging support, he enacted huge tax cuts to mollify and further enrich the already wealthy and powerful to assure their ongoing obeyance.

The ascendancy of the free world's supposed leader was in stark contrast to that of the czar, who was slowly losing his once iron grip on governance. There had been a time when the people had spoken and the choice had been made to accept scarcity versus abundance. But scarcity continued far longer than promised, and all Russians, especially the youth, were protesting in increasing numbers. To restore his former luster and widespread popularity, the czar knew something major must happen if he wanted to regain preeminence. A victory decided by winning the most rounds was not nearly enough; what he needed was a decisive knockout.

For him, the answer was obvious, and it would play well to the long-standing Russian nationalistic psyche. There would be nothing like soundly defeating all that America represented to rehabilitate his diminishing approval ratings. Cyberwarfare was the perfect weapon—a time bomb that gathered increasing strength due to the fears of the American people. Because ongoing ineptitude at the White House was a sure bet, ruination would occur while America's president fumbled and its Congress fiddled.

Other leaders of repressive regimes were already in the czar's pocket and could be counted on to provoke America and distract Washington from the real danger. Occasional testing of their missiles, confiscation of American-flagged oil tankers, and keeping the bevy of Middle East pots boiling to strain the financial and military resources of the United States would be small prices to pay for America's effective demise. Not surprisingly, the czar found it easy to befriend the fanatical lunatics hell-bent on the destruction of all things American because the terrorists weren't accountable to anybody and respected no country borders. Getting conventional military armament into the hands of those who abhorred the US was by intention, and using Cherkov as a conduit had been profitable beyond his imagination. However, the czar wanted no part in providing help with developing anything that approached nuclear or biological capabilities. Though championing such ambitions, neither Russia nor the Chinese would ever allow other regimes to achieve such a goal.

Hap had long ago determined that Russia was no longer driving the bus as it hadn't and couldn't keep pace with China's two decades of double-digit growth in military spending. Once invincible, America had become vulnerable for the same reason. Apart from failing to adequately fund a national defense, America could no longer guarantee that its aging computer systems, which managed everything, could not be compromised. Not only the missiles but also the silos that held them were from a bygone era, and no one knew if they could even get aloft. Even if so, the nation's Minuteman arsenal had been essentially buried for more than fifty years without testing their nuclear payloads. Unreliable equipment coupled with the lack of enlightened leadership in Washington could prove dangerous and devastatingly so. It wasn't much different from lowering the drawbridge, inviting the enemy in, and conceding the castle by handing over a full set of keys to it. Such a concession would be seen by the rest of the world as nothing more than a carte-blanche unconditional surrender without so much as a skirmish.

Russia's economy still suffered from having fueled the Soviet surge in the nuclear arms race of the 1970s. The collapse of the USSR caused by that race had enabled other countries to prosper, and the czar wanted payback from the West. All would have gone according to plan had Hap Franklin not been a distraction. Cherkov was unable to move on without closure, and until that was achieved, he would remain mired in his personal purgatory. The old psychological wounds he had received at Hap's hands continued to fester, and he could not refrain from picking at the mental scar tissue. Cherkov desperately wanted what he considered his rightful revenge; he was obsessed with getting it, and he assumed that this time, the somewhat compromised czar would not interfere.

TRUMPING THE TRUTH

THE RUSSIANS' JOB WAS ACCOMMODATED by an American president who had quickly lost his entertainment value soon after being elected. The only visible evidence of his work was limited to incessant tweets that served only as accelerants for the flaming rage of his rabid followers. Beyond the disciples of hate, his support base included the downtrodden about whom he had no real knowledge or direct contact with but was masterful at manipulating. He knew what they were thinking but could not articulate, so he did it for them by echoing their innermost fears and biases.

Privately, he remained aloof from the needs of those who had put him in office. His cocksure but reckless and rampant actions paved the way for continued foreign interference with American democracy. The lasting damage went beyond influencing his own election. Each day of his term in office, he tested the endurance of a bewildered republic by exhibiting a stunning level of incompetence. Four years was generally a sensible interval for measuring results, but the jury came in far ahead of schedule by clamoring for his ouster almost from the onset. Even with the passage of time, historians would all agree that this presidency would forever be defined as an ugly and dangerous epoch in the country's history.

For the czar, the role of Paradiso was simply a logical extension of the deceit that further nourished the seeds of discontent sown daily by the leader of the free world. When harnessed to spread widespread disinformation, Paradiso could be the first volley to soften up America for the czar's grand scheme. Voter fatigue and political exasperation amid a faltering economy made it easy to undermine confidence in the election process. Saturating the airwaves with propaganda intended to warp the political narrative, undermine the media, hack voting systems, and corrupt databases with malignant viruses was just the beginning. In time, other hostages would include the energy grid and Wall Street trading platforms. After financial institutions faltered, massive intrusions of malicious attacks would hobble America's entire infrastructural integrity. Partnering with China, supply chains of the essential goods America needed but no longer produced would be disrupted until the pain could no longer be tolerated.

Audacious as it might seem, the czar was convinced that he could create a perfect storm of revolution all by himself and that in time, his reign of tyranny would extend to the West. Delusional as it might sound if spoken aloud, he privately believed it to be his personal manifest destiny. A new world order with him at the helm was not as far-fetched as some might have thought. Plus, given Russia's diminishing economic ability to maintain its one-time fearsome military complex, his choice of spreading discord electronically was a far cheaper way to infiltrate and destabilize the West.

The pandemic response bungled by the same sitting president had confirmed America's dependence on China to produce virtually all products including some critical medicines. Reliance on another nation's manufacturing monopoly was dangerous and stupid. Unprecedented demand without supply would eventually cripple if not vanquish the czar's sworn enemy.

Since about the time he had come to prominence, the czar had watched from afar while a greedy America had stumbled along amid growing prosperity by outsourcing its economic independence. The czar saw this as a harbinger of what the future held for democracy. It was time to unleash the second of Cherkov's major assaults. Bankrupting the captains of American industry would weaken their resolve to rebuild the economy; they would be mired in despair. Though most would eventually crawl back from the edge, some would take the plunge from a rooftop. Finally, the pandemonium he had patiently awaited would arrive and his sovereignty extended. He even had a name for his multipronged plan—Operation Suffocation of Freedom.

Ruling aristocracies inevitably failed. Beyond the czar's predecessors, the collapsed Romanov dynasty, any observer had to look no further than the French and American Revolutions for proof of that. Even the once mighty British Empire had been reduced to a constitutional monarchy with an impotent sovereign. There, the royal family's pomp and circumstance was largely a sideshow staged for tourists.

A second civil war was brewing across the land of the free and onetime home of the brave. If properly stoked, it would result in the same class warfare that had toppled all others through history. For the time being, the czar would continue feeding the American president's ego, knowing it was premature to challenge his supremacy until the timing was ripe for a takeover and hoping it might be one that need not necessarily be hostile. Besides, after several years in office but still bereft of any sensibility, the American president had yet to stray beyond the frontier of ignorance, and that would not likely change.

Beyond his failure to address systemic racism and manage a concerted response to the coronavirus, the president's mismanagement of other national catastrophes had been handled in the same way. Though flummoxed by his lack of sense or purpose, POTUS's savvy White House handlers soon became adept at only one thing—playing the blame game by diffusing and redirecting all criticism. Instead of doing their jobs by engaging in ideological debate, the completely dumbfounded and nonplussed members of Congress were rendered impotent by fear of reprisal from Pennsylvania Avenue.

Some feared the possibility that the once great American experiment had run its course and that the country would never again be a beacon of hope and encouragement to the world. Increasing polarization of the electorate spelled trouble ahead if voters again failed to get off their asses when they next had the chance. If not, the passing of America's dominance as the civilized world leader would assuredly happen by default. One of the lowest voter participation rates of any modern democracy was downright disgraceful; fewer than half of Americans had exercised that right during the last election. As citizens of the world's oldest democratic republic, it was shameful and embarrassing that so many failed to see the significance of their duty.

Absent bold leadership, the coronavirus was the first widespread test of America's determination to defend itself in a generation. Unaccustomed to sacrifice and in contrast to the rest of the world, America quickly punted; instant self-gratification triumphed over science and reason. Following a few short months of self-isolation, many grew weary of sacrifice and could not resist the allure of the beaches. In defiance of medical science, those who prematurely crowded into bars and restaurants or attended rallies paid the ultimate price, but so did those who acted responsibly. The lack of an orderly federal response did not go unnoticed by the rest of the world, whose confidence had been on the wane ever since the president had taken office.

The president's audacity fueled by his ongoing horrendous, farcical, and narcissistic behavior extended through the ranks of his flunkies, who in their own ways all contributed to undermining the bedrock of democracy. The promise of universal prosperity resulted in more economic disparity. Growing social unrest—always a precursor to future political violence elsewhere in the world—was a more alarming wake-up call. Some of the president's disciples who believed America should no longer be a stranger to anarchy had begun taking abhorrent actions to bring about what many feared would be an inevitable societal collapse.

Most believed in their hearts that he was unfit and the wrong occupant of the Oval Office long before the impeachment proceedings, but they worried more about the specter of a second term. Thankfully, that was never to be. Following his resounding defeat by the voters, his weaponized rhetoric on social media proved more menacing when he was a toxic lame duck. His goal was to create havoc and instability by destroying the political ecosystem. Given a complicit attorney general and sympathetic Supreme Court, the world expected that America's electoral integrity would be challenged once he lost. Even after dozens of lawsuits contesting the vote had been dismissed, a final obstacle was simply removing the buffoon from office.

Following a second impeachment two weeks before his term ended, most expected a resignation and subsequent pardon by his vice president, but the chicanery continued unabated. One possible scenario considered by many in closed-door meetings was an unprecedented but temporary military coup d'état that would physically oust him from the people's house. Fortunately, such drastic action was not required.

THE SLEEPING DRAGON

I T CAME AS NO SURPRISE TO LANGLEY that Beijing took a back seat to what they already knew the czar was up to. The Russian leader was in a hurry and desperately wanted America's collapse to happen under his watch and direction whereas China had learned from history that the ultimate spoils of war went to those who were patient. Even as the inventor of gunpowder more than a thousand years ago, China had limited its use to fireworks until the right time. With nearly four thousand years of written history and as the oldest living civilization on planet Earth, the Chinese understood the importance of patience. When asked about the significance of the French Revolution of 1789, Zhou Enlai, the first premier of the Peoples' Republic of China, or PRC, responded that after the passing of only two hundred years—about the duration of America's independence—it was "too soon to say."

Unlike the largely symbolic border walls quickly erected by America in recent times, the Great Wall of China had taken thousands of years to build, but it too was not secure. Unable to keep out barbarian nomads such as the Mongols under the marauding conqueror Genghis Khan, it had been reduced to a disintegrating symbol of strength in spite of its attraction for tourists.

The Chinese were no strangers to dynastic rule having survived, grown, and prospered beginning two thousand years before Christ. The imperial rule by kings and emperors included some names familiar to the West even though most Americans were ignorant of history. What they knew about China was largely limited to chopsticks, Kung Fu, takeout food, coolie slippers, and fortune cookies.

Maybe America's reluctance to recognize China as the world's engine and economic powerhouse stemmed from its embarrassment that it had erred in ceding that role to China. The downfall of nations usually occurred by a confluence of factors—fear, scarcity, the lack of conviction, and a willingness to adapt. China's president was not an archetypical monarch; he knew a proud America would need more time to adapt, and he was more than willing to wait. He also knew better than to provoke outright open conflict.

The Chinese understood that war never determined who was right, only who was left. Annihilation of their Western adversary wouldn't best serve their plan because China depended on America's voracious appetite for its prodigious output. Anything China didn't have or couldn't manufacture could be purchased as it had been for some time. China had amassed a huge portfolio of prime American real estate, and its enormous holdings of precious metals, vast mineral deposits, and other essential raw materials elsewhere on the planet would assure its manufacturing capabilities and thereby economic world dominance for all time. Its global ascent seemed all but inevitable and unstoppable. Though Japan was called the house of the rising sun, in time, it would be China that would assert its agenda and impose a new order wherever the sun shone, and that would be a bad moon arising.

Few were better at reading the tea leaves than Hap. When pressed, even the seventh floor at Langley begrudgingly acknowledged that his premonitions usually came true. A dozen years earlier, he had written a position paper that foreshadowed what he believed was the ultimate threat to America the beautiful. It had nothing to do with nuclear or pandemic annihilation but all about economic enslavement. Though forwarded up the chain to the NSA, it had not been given the priority it should have received, so there had been as usual no response. But every year since, the Chinese continued to move forward and fulfill Hap's prophecy. It began with the very best of America's universities educating and preparing China's youth for what was ahead. The real kicker was that many of those were granted full scholarships as an allurement.

Of greater consequence was the outright theft of Yankee technology and intellectual property, which was a multipronged assault. It began with stealing industrial and manufacturing know-how and then moved on to include ripping off patented secrets in chemistry, medicine, and electronic wizardry. Whatever couldn't be legally acquired was simply siphoned off or stolen. All along, they had quietly fielded the world's largest standing army without raising much alarm from other countries.

No matter whether it would appear a friendly or passive take-over, this was not a scenario Hap could abide or was willing to permit playing out in front of his son and daughter or any subsequent generations. Though such a specter was hardly something he or anyone else could vigorously reject, it was not just a premonition Hap would blithely accept. He knew the dragon would prove impossible to slay, but might be forced into hibernation for a while longer.

SETTING THE STAGE

ABOVE ALL ELSE, INVESTORS HATED UNCERTAINTY. It was no different with the intelligence community. Market turbulence was good only for short-term traders, not long-term investors. There were simply far too many wild cards that could derail the engines of growth. The scant rise in the standard of living for the few was more than offset by a general decline for the majority. After reviewing the gauges of economic activity and consumer sentiment, Wall Street placed its bets, which was nothing more than front-running the same wagers made by the masses. Small investors never seemed to recognize what was often nothing beyond yet another daisy chain of events that wouldn't work out the way they'd hoped.

What the market yearned for was a strong, sustained dose of certainty like the prolonged prosperity of the postwar period of Hap's youth. Unfortunately, that would never again be the norm. In its place was uncertainty, which spawned speculation motivated by greed alone. Early in life, Hap had found that the result of putting short-term self-interest aside ultimately produced much higher returns over time. Those who hadn't adopted such a principle would learn a harsh lesson much like the aftermath of Holland's tulip mania in 1637.

The czar's timing could not have been better. It would begin with minor disruptions to the electronic trading platforms followed by a total collapse. Besides plummeting stock prices, much-needed capital formation would be virtually impossible. Washington would try to fix it with yet another stimulus package, which only pushed the burden further down the road to an unsuspecting new generation of paupers whose knees would buckle beneath the weight of increased taxes. Distrust of big government was becoming a universal pastime. Federal public expenditures of this nature angered Hap and for good reason.

To create economic equality, the tax code was nothing more than an inefficient mechanism for transferring wealth from people who did something to people who didn't. National defense exigencies notwithstanding, the arguments for limited government spending were unassailable. The ongoing pillaging of taxpayers would soon escalate beyond their ability to pay, which would invite real revolt and revolution. With its confidence shaken, a disabled America would have no choice but to embark on a path from which there was no turning back.

America's intelligence-gathering colossus now comprised more than a dozen agencies with at least 100,000 on its combined payrolls and commanded a colossal $60 billion annual budget. More was larded into the dark arts of covert warfare through other public troughs and co-opted from the military, but only a few in Congress knew for sure how much that was.

Since the trio of terrorist attacks by al-Qaeda on 9/11, the United States had spent half a trillion dollars to prevent such a thing from ever happening again. Despite its resources and hardened resolve, the vast constellation of spy agencies wouldn't see it coming the next time either. Hap had seen it from the other side when involved in toppling repressive regimes his country found distasteful. The CIA's arsenal wasn't limited to weaponry; it always contained a mixed bag of tricks—including sabotage. Often, Hap's role had been setting the stage for a violent insurgency to help usher in some law and order amid the ensuing chaos typically through a military coup. It was America's turn, and its plight was not much different from those it had corrupted overseas.

Hap had known all along that the United States had more to fear from the dragon than the bear, but to defeat the Russians at their own game, it was first necessary to put the dragon back to sleep for a long time. There was one Western attribute that neither the Russians nor the Chinese could ever replicate—ingenuity. Their people had been brainwashed for so long that they had lost the imagination to figure a clever way out as an American or German might. Obliging, blind obedience to autocratic rule was imbedded in the psyche, and much as pernicious, systemic racism was in the United States, it would need yet another generation or two to flush out.

The despotic leaders of these nations were a breed of dogs far different from those they ruled, and Hap had gotten to know one of them better than he had wanted to. He had bested Dmitri Cherkov before, and he was counting on doing so one last time.

PART IV:
Intermezzo

PACKING UP AND SHIPPING OUT

ACKING WAS A RITUAL, and after doing so nearly every week for thirty years when traveling on business, Hap was good at it. After an abundance of forethought, he executed it quickly and with precision; he had packed just enough, never too much, clothing to see him through a trip. Some of the other stuff could have been optional, but it wasn't. There were very few things in life that Hap could not do without. The most important of those was his morning coffee but made only the way he liked it—boldly roasted with a dash of cinnamon and freshly ground nutmeg. If ranked among the bare essentials for travel, his nutmeg grinder would top spare underwear and a change of socks. As to the amount of needed nutmeg itself, that too was calibrated in advance. He knew that when grated, a whole nutmeg provided about three teaspoons of goodness, more than enough for the trip to Italy.

Beyond the aviator sunglasses, another essential was a practical but fashionable hat. Apart from preventing overexposure to the sun, a good hat also appeased Hap's vanity by concealing his thinning hair. Only one hat from his vast collection of wide-brimmed Borsalino and Stetson fedoras had been spared in the fire. Fortunately, it had been kept in the stable, but it was the one he would have chosen anyway. The hand-blocked lightweight straw Panama had been custom made for him by the world's oldest and most distinguished hatter. Lock & Co. on London's St. James's Street had been around since 1676 and had learned a thing or two along the way about making fine hats. A royal warrant holder,

Lock had been the choice of British monarchs for generations and for good reason.

The special gear Hap had ordered from Bud that couldn't pass through the TSA screening would be waiting for him on the other side. Hap hoped he wouldn't need it, but until he might, the weaponry would be hidden from Weezie. This was supposed to be a vacation from the usual things that went bump in the night, and try as he might to forget about the jeopardy ahead, Hap knew he couldn't and wouldn't. Atop the short list of things that could dominate Hap's zest for life was Cherkov, who could play the spoiler. For Weezie's sake, Hap was unwilling to let that happen just yet.

Packed for the next morning's flight to Dulles, Hap gave into the temptation to take a drive through the borough that had been prompted by a foreboding that it might be his last opportunity to do so. Since the fire, he had been sleeping in the stable, the aroma of which had somehow grounded him to the soil of Mother Earth. He liked the feeling of getting back to the plain and simpler life of his people, who through time had kept the implicit bargain they had made with the earth under their feet.

While meandering the roughly eight square miles that comprised the enclave of entitlement known as Fox Chapel, Hap suspected that damn few of its residents concerned themselves with ameliorating the plight of those less fortunate. Rather, and with rabid zeal, their focus was limited on only things befitting their station such as tax-avoidance schemes, intergenerational wealth transfer, restocking their wine cellars, and getting an early tee time.

No matter where the comma fell in their seven-or eight-figure net worths, they were united by something else—an unspoken but terrifying fear, a recurring nightmare of a future that might inject hand-to-hand combat into inevitable class warfare. The indifference and arrogance of wealth were easy to spot. Hap noticed that the absurd response of a few who lived secluded and pampered lives in the largest estates had been to post *Black Lives Matter* signs. Though visible from the road, they were located well outside the imposing driveway gates and perimeter fencing purportedly erected to keep the deer away.

Fox Chapel probably could afford one, but it had no standing army to mount a defense if such a collective nightmare ever came to pass. Instead, the borough's unofficial plan relied on several of its residents who had made a friend in the White House. Given ongoing support and campaign contributions, that friend would dispatch a federal militia to turn back any assault on their way of life. Clearly, these were not Hap's people, and maybe, he thought, it was time to ship out for good.

TRANSATLANTIC TANGO

H AP WAS ANYTHING BUT HAPHAZARD, especially when it came to travel arrangements. Since he was flying from Pittsburgh, the plan was to meet Weezie at the gate at Dulles. That wasn't his favorite place from which to embark when traveling internationally, but it would be far easier on Weezie than having her add another leg to JFK.

After checking in and zipping through the preclearance line at security, he spied her sitting alone though her face was hidden behind a magazine. Betrayed by her long legs crossed in the familiar way he found so provocative, she had always been easy to identify if hard to catch. Hap had been trying for a long time, and was of the mind that he might even close the deal on that trip. And if not, the pursuit itself provided plenty of motivation for the next time. Consumed by whatever she was reading, she wasn't aware of his arrival until he was standing over her and staring down her blouse.

"I feel your gaze, Mr. Franklin, even if it's focused on my girls."

"Well, Dr. Porter, since they're designed more for tactile inspection, just wait till you feel my touch."

"Shame on you, Hap. You've really never experienced contrition, have you?"

"Contrition? Isn't that something like remorse? Either way, can't say I'm at all familiar with the concept."

"No wonder as they're second cousins to humility—another trait missing from your gene pool."

"I'll remember to mention all these shortcomings to my primary care physician."

"Tell him the diagnosis was made by a world-class shrink who should've charged you an outrageous co-pay."

"He may rightly ask if you made any curative recommendations."

"Hap, if you were a real patient of mine, I'd put a monkey wrench to your head and give it a huge tug."

"I can think of other things you could tug at that would yield a faster and far more satisfactory ending."

"Facetious and flippant to the end. Honestly, Hap, you're overdue for some required penitence, so sit down and behave yourself."

He leaned down and delivered a longer and sloppier kiss than he should have in such a public arena. Though he enjoyed their banter, when it got too close to the bone and approached trading outright insults, he often chose to pacify her in that fashion.

Weary from the mostly sleepless prior week of preparation, Hap slumped into the seat beside her, and until the flight was called, they talked only of the adventure that was in store for them. Italy and particularly Tuscany would be the ideal place for the getaway they desperately needed. Despite her pleading over the last few weeks, Hap would not reveal their precise destination or answer any questions about the itinerary. He wanted it to remain a surprise until arrival and had taken desperate measures to make it so. He knew she would be utterly overwhelmed, and that would be his reward.

Luckily for Hap, Louise left her purse and belongings under his care when she went to the restroom; he was able to swap out her passport for the nearly identical one Bud had provided. A cursory comparison of all the pages and stamps confirmed they were alike in every way, even the dog-eared and worn edges. The falsified documents along with a stash of worn euros had arrived only the day before, and to Hap's surprise and horror, by FedEx, which was akin to but hardly as secure as the diplomatic pouch he was used to from a bygone era. That possible breach notwithstanding, so far, everything had gone as planned, and that was the way he liked it.

Preboarding for first-class passengers was a benefit all by itself; Hap hated to stand in line for anything. One of the reasons he had chosen Air France was its use of the extra-wide-bodied aircraft that featured forward compartments that accommodated two generous side-by-side lounging berths on each side of the aisle. His familiarity with how they could best be used for sleeping once the private curtain was drawn was the result of having flown millions of miles during his career.

Having witnessed more real estate from the sky than some pilots had, Hap insisted that Weezie take the window seat, which she was thrilled to do. Since it was an overnight flight, she would view the takeoff from Washington and the early morning landing in Paris before making the short connection to Florence. If the usual flight pattern were followed, the descent into Florence would provide Weezie a breathtaking panorama of what Toscana would be like over the next week.

Though KLM offered a somewhat shorter and far cheaper flight that connected through Amsterdam, Hap preferred Air France for its amenities. The French knew how to coddle its passengers especially when they were paying big-time for the ride. Besides, as Hap's father had been fond of saying, "Remember, son, it's only money, and if you're resourceful, you can always get more of it." His father had never explained the nuts and bolts of how that was done, but it obviously had been impactful if Hap still remembered those words. With such sage advice and taking his cue from the French, Hap intended to pamper Weezie beyond her already heightened expectations.

After the long climb-out to reach cruising altitude, the attendants began offering an impressive array of appetizers and beverages. Beyond the assortment of fruit, caviar, pâtés, and foie gras, Weezie managed to finish two glasses of a buttery chardonnay, and that soon showed in her growing playfulness. The meal selection was more than acceptable and no doubt a far cry from the chow being slung for the poor bastards back in steerage. Weezie chose the duck confit, and Hap, already thinking of Tuscany, the veal scaloppini al limone. Dessert proved to be an easy choice too.

"You know, Weeze, given your typical resistance to desserts of any kind and resolution to never gain an ounce, I'm surprised that you requested the flourless chocolate cake."

"Oh Hap, don't you remember what you said after our first French kiss in Bar Harbor?"

"Of course. I said it was like plunging my tongue into the warm, gooey center of just such a cake."

"My, I love how you describe everything in life with such articulatory precision."

"It's the wannabe author in me."

"Well, just this once, I'm off diet in remembrance of those very words."

"Then I hope you'll give me another taste once you have a mouthful."

"Only if you do the same with your gelato."

"Done, and with no further encouragement required."

"You know, Hap, I've always wondered if there'd be the same earthy magnetism between us if we'd met as complete strangers."

"Probably more. You know how the mind craves and the body aches for a novel and willing partner. In fact, I think some men call it getting some strange."

"Lordy, have you always been so bad?"

"Pretty much, and it's only occasionally limited by the poverty of my imagination."

"I'm glad I didn't know that back in high school though I had my suspicions."

"Too bad you never verified them."

"Perhaps one day I'll catch up. Then again, the problem with that is there are way too many things going on inside that twisted head of yours about which I am still unaware."

"Yeah Weeze, it's getting to be a very crowded space up there, but one day you'll figure it all out. You did go to school for that, right?"

"You bet I did, but I suspect you'll keep it all inside for the forensic pathologist to unravel during the postmortem."

Once all the whims of those seated in the forward cabin were addressed, the walled curtains surrounding the berths were pulled shut for privacy. Some would watch a movie while others tried to sleep, but all would be wearing the complimentary noise-canceling headphones and welcome the silence.

Hap had another option in mind. As always, he was having a hard time keeping his hands off her but knew he had to wait until the lights were dimmed and the rest of their cabin mates had settled in for a nap. He figured that copping a cheap feel in the light of day wasn't nearly as adventuresome as groping all of her in the dark. Weezie must have been thinking the same thing, but her thoughts about what might happen next were far more modest than his. Hap had something in store for her the likes of which she could never have imagined.

"Hap, I don't think we've ever spent the night in twin beds before."

"I have a little surprise for you. I bet you didn't know these can be converted to a double by removing the sideboard arm that separates them."

"And how did you come by *that* information?"

"Lots of advance research, but tonight, it'll be old-fashioned, practical trial and error."

"Oh that's right. I forgot you were trained to figure stuff like this out."

Hap quickly and expertly lowered and stowed the barrier between the berths.

"There. See how that works?"

"You seem well practiced in dismantling things that get in your way, Hap, and you know what? I've always admired that in a man."

"Good to know. Now why don't you move a little closer to my side so we can whisper a few secrets in each other's ears without disturbing our neighbors?"

"Okay, but you're beginning to look way too pleased with yourself, so you'd better mind your manners."

"Weeze, you know I don't like change, right? Well, I like relevancy even less."

"Then revert to your usual bad manners and do what you must, Hap, but try being discreet."

"And what if I don't subscribe to Shakespeare's notion that discretion is the better part of valor?"

"Can't say I'd blame you, Hap. If I were you, I'd want me too."

Her firm, full breasts beckoned, but he knew the problem with that. Undressing her even under a blanket was a boundary he would not likely succeed in crossing. Hap knew the limits of propriety, and for the most part, he had always obeyed the rules … except when it came to Weezie. The plan he had in mind was less daring and much safer from discovery. Besides, invading her most private place in such a public space would make for a far better memory. It was a long shot, but Hap liked the odds and put his plan in motion. Weezie felt his hand move slowly up her leg as their tender and quiet kissing grew more passionate, but when Hap began exploring the inside of her thigh, she hesitated.

"Hap, you gotta be kidding! Here? You can't be serious."

"I do like to kid, but I'm always serious, and this is one of those times of a lifetime."

"Really?"

"Really, and because you're wearing a skirt, this should be an easy decision. You'll have to be quieter than usual, though, and try not to use the Lord's name when your time comes."

"Right, I wouldn't want to startle the others, but if things get out of hand, don't think I won't push the call button."

It was a foregone conclusion. They both knew all along she would relent, but only after enjoying the humorous verbal foreplay, which was an enduring hallmark of their relationship. Even in the near darkness, Hap saw her sly grin. Weezie drew one leg up to make it easy for him to find what he was after, and he was soon rewarded by her acquiescence. He probed her slowly and gingerly at first, then increased the tempo, and finally settled into a penetrating rhythm until his fingers were bathed in a dewy dampness.

Her time arrived sooner than expected, and then came a second and third as Hap continued his work, which proved a fitting coda to what had come before. Prone to outbursts in such situations, Weezie found it difficult to stifle the ecstasy she always experienced when Hap took her to new heights. Her eyes dilated as if cued while her entire body remained aquiver. Soon, any residual tension from her job and life back home melted away. Her body limp, she remained motionless while savoring every moment of the precious aftermath. Soon, the muffled panting ran its course. Dr. Porter was now officially on vacation, and it showed.

"That was some undertaking, Hap."

"Thank you, Weeze. I'm always game to get down under with you for a taking. Think of it as a remedial exercise in reawakening your desire."

"From your grin, which right now makes you look like a mule eating briars, I'm guessing you're seeking my ex post facto consent for that little innovative move."

"Thanks for the acknowledgment, Weeze, but no applause is necessary, especially in front of the other passengers."

"You really do know how to excite a girl."

"I've made it my life's work, and I've perhaps just proven beyond any doubt that idle hands are indeed the devil's mischief."

"One wouldn't ever find idle hands in your workshop. You know, Hap, you're incorrigible, and I should have known that in seventh grade."

"You must have guessed that way back then or you wouldn't have played so hard to get all these years."

"Truth is, I did speculate what it might be like with you, and that was long before you became such an accomplished undercover man."

"I wish you'd acted on those adolescent impulses."

"Think of this trip as catch-up, Hap, and I hope you can keep up."

"I've never failed to keep my end up."

"That doesn't surprise me. It's no wonder you're so sought after by Team USA. Is that due to the kind of sleight-of-hand work you just demonstrated or all manner of deception?"

"Damn, I'd always figured it was the sparkling eyes or the cut of my jib."

"Maybe that too, but for me, it all begins with your hungry bedroom eyes."

"And right now, they're ravenous."

"All right, enough, Hap. On your feet. I need to go to the bathroom."

"Well then, let me show you the way."

"I'm quite capable of handling this on my own. Plus, I need to change my panties thanks to you."

"No need to thank me, Weeze. It's all part of the service in this compartment."

"Don't you dare follow me. I mean it, Hap."

"But it takes two to tango."

She could tell what he had in mind from the devilish look that suddenly spread across his face. He had always wanted a smidgen more than he was entitled to, and when he combined his infectious smile and engaging hazel eyes, Hap had captivated her heart since that first slow dance in junior high. For those and so many other reasons, she decided to continue sparring with him for the sheer fun of it.

"Look, there's no way I'm punching your ticket for membership in the mile-high club and especially in a public toilet."

"But Weeze, I'm told it's dues-free for life if earned over the ocean. Plus I was hoping to begin our vacation with a bang."

"Have you always had such a rapacious and nearly canine appetite for sex?"

"Only since learning it was the ultimate panacea for all of life's troubles."

"So you're one of those perils in the night I should be wary of?"

"Were it not for that, I'd be a pretty boring guy."

"Hap, you're implacable. Have you ever considered that you might have too many plans but maybe not enough dreams?"

When she returned, it was clear the wine was taking its toll because she grew more amorous once under the shared blanket. Hap would have been content to just doze off with her in his arms, but she had other ideas. Her kisses were full of passion, and using one and then both hands, she teased him to full attention.

"Turnabout's only fair, Hap, and after centuries of men feeling entitled to women's bodies in an unfettered manner, it's about time we women turned the tables on you men."

"I'd be the last man to ever deny women unrestricted access to my body."

"Great, because it's now your turn to refrain from crying out."

"Actually, I'm doing so now by hiding my excitement over the pleasant sensation that seems to be coming from somewhere down below."

"In that case, maybe I should loosen your belt, undo your pants, and unzip them to see if that helps."

"You're the doctor. I'm guessing you've made a definitive diagnosis."

"Oh yes, Hap, and I'm thinking of applying the same remedy we've used before."

"I can't argue with that, especially given the past success of its surefire result."

"Nor should you argue, especially about a sure thing as you guys call it, unless you're worried that lowering your expectations might lead to a decrease in performance."

After pulling the blanket over her head for cover, she slid down to find the source of his feigned discomfort, but she took her time getting there. Even in the darkness, her geographically sensitive tongue needed no direction to its destination. As Hap hoped she might, Weezie chose an extended route as opposed to the shortcut that most others might choose to follow. It was the same well-worn path that had proven so successful on prior journeys down Hap's landscape.

Finally, and with the able assistance of both hands, she worked her magic like no other. To Hap, it seemed he had never before known such arousal. The eruption didn't take long, and after unleashing its fury, she brought him to a fitting conclusion. Only when the involuntary convulsions ended did she release him and emerge from under the blanket to reveal her own smile of smug satisfaction.

"So Hap, I'm betting you won't find such creature comforts in coach class."

"Or on a Greyhound bus, my dear, so thank you for making the skies a lot friendlier."

"I'm happy to help, Hap, and I hope you'll finally check that off your bucket list."

"Actually, I brought that list along. It's a long one but well hidden in my checked luggage."

"Well, I'd like to examine it and maybe before you unpack anything else."

"That's not a good idea, Weeze. You might gasp at what's yet to come."

"Given your epicurean lifestyle, probably not."

Hap knew it was going to be a vacation like no other. More important, he wasn't about to spoil it too soon by telling her about the imminent danger ahead.

TUSCAN LAVENDER

ECAUSE OF A LIFETIME OF SAVING, salvaging, and at times scrimping, Hap believed he was entitled to an occasional extravagance, and this vacation was going to be one of them. It was a good thing Weezie had heeded his advice to pack sparingly as there was not much room for luggage in the Maserati. Though Hap no longer drove as fast as he once had, he nevertheless liked knowing that an overabundance of horsepower was there and ready to respond on demand. In this instance, he also knew it could easily outrun anything on the road that might chase him, and that included Cherkov.

Prior to his picking it up, the fast car had been outfitted by an advance team for any special road hazards or emergencies. Beyond several grenades in the driver's side pouch, concealed under the trunk mat were two of man's best friends—a Sig Sauer P230 and a Walther PPK together with plenty of ammo. Bud had long ago stopped asking why Hap always requested two weapons when one would have sufficed. Though similar and capable of getting the same job done, Hap knew and appreciated the subtle, nuanced distinctions between the two weapons. To him, selecting guns was no different from choosing any other tool; as when laboring in the garden, he had certain preferences for tools suitable for the tasks he might face in the line of duty. After working together for so many years, Bud had ceased being surprised by Hap's whims, knowing he was choosy about all things.

Whereas the vehicles Hap had trained in at the Farm for evasive driving were Chevys and Fords, not Maseratis, the techniques and maneuvers were transferable, so he was certain that no harm would befall them on their way to Bucine. It was about an hour's drive through the rich and fertile Tuscan hills. Once outside Florence, there was little in the landscape that indicated human inhabitance—just unspoiled scenery.

Hap was somewhat familiar with the route to Bucine and their ultimate destination of Tenuta di Lupinari, but the navigation system was helpful in keeping him on track to arrive by nightfall. The splendor of the Lupinari estate was breathtaking. The long, private road was unmarked in order to keep any onlookers out. The first marvel was passing through what must have been fifty acres of solid sunflowers before reaching the mammoth gates, where Hap was greeted by name. He had been there before with Kate on several occasions, and it was apparent that the employees had good memories of the impression he had made as well as the generous gratuities spread among them.

Proceeding up the mile-long driveway was an enchanting experience as well and particularly when the castle's tower came into view. Lined by dozens of majestic Mediterranean cypress trees, the winding stone roadbed traversed a hilly terrain covered with grapevines of all varieties. It wasn't uncommon for cypress trees to live more than a thousand years in such a climate, and some of these might be a testament to such longevity. Hap tried to imagine what they had witnessed over such a span of time. As they neared the crest of the mountain, they beheld magnificent olive groves bathed in the shimmering crimson and golden sunset. As he had hoped, Weezie was spellbound by it all.

Antonio Pellegrino, a renowned and successful builder from Rome, had purchased what was once an Italian nobleman's sprawling compound. After investing a huge sum to bring the castle back to its former grandeur for his family and convert the once ramshackle outbuildings into luxurious, unique guest quarters, he then restored the fields, vineyards, and grounds. Following a period of ten or so years for the transformation to a working estate and winery, Lupinari finally opened to a very select and discerning group of patrons from around the world. Like Hap, after a first visit, all would return, and some did again and again.

Due to its relative isolation and dearth of acceptable places to dine nearby, two meals were available daily. A bountiful breakfast buffet was open to all, and dinner, by reservation only, was indeed a sumptuous experience that rivaled the world's best restaurants. The Pellegrino family's wines were exceptional, including the complimentary house variety that was available all day for the tasting and taking. Hap was fussy about wine; he would rather drink a cup of hemlock than the swill most American restaurants offered as their house wines. In his opinion, they were much like the so-called fresh fruit juices now fabricated in a lab.

Antonio had passed since Hap's last visit, but his widow had marshalled on without him to fulfill his abiding dream of Lupinari becoming a world-class destination. She had an exceptionally discriminating eye for detail, and every day, she suggested an idea to the staff that would make something better than it had been. If in America, she might have been called persnickety, but that's what was demanded here when catering to the privileged few who had discovered this oasis.

Signora Pellegrino was well educated and sophisticated; she was once also as stunning a woman as Hap had ever known. Though doubtful she would ever again marry, she was widely considered among the fairest and most sought after of Tuscan dowagers. Some in her innermost circle called her contessa, and Hap had always thought it a perfect description. Tuscan women had always held an abiding fascination for him, and there were countless reasons why.

It was a long-standing custom for special guests of Tenuta Lupinari to be welcomed personally by a Pellegrino family member, and in Hap's case, it would be the matriarch herself. She was awaiting his arrival in the castle's great room, and she rose quickly to greet him with a genuine hug followed by kisses on both cheeks. As he had anticipated, the contessa exuded the ideal combination of grace tinged with just the right amount of noblesse oblige. In her case, aristocracy was an attitude, a noble gesture, not an entitlement over which to gloat.

Since first becoming aware of Hap's reservations and knowing that his wife, Kate, had died tragically a few years earlier, the contessa had wondered who might be accompanying him. Knowing Hap as she did, she knew it could not possibly be some vapid, buxom babe; she had imagined that she might be a younger version of Kate. After all, it was what men did these days the second or third time around, and he wouldn't be the first to hook up with a nubile woman younger than his children. She was relieved and pleased to see that his companion appeared to be neither of those. Recalling that he had spoken some Italian, and probably to test him, she began in a mixture of both their native tongues.

"Benvenuto, Signor Franklin, or should I say bentornato?"

"Yes ma'am, I guess 'Welcome back' is the right greeting for me."

"And who is this bella donna, Hap?"

"Signora Pellegrino, meet my good friend, Dr. Louise Porter."

Weezie offered her hand, which Mrs. Pellegrino graciously clasped in hers. "It's so nice to finally meet you, signora, but based on what Hap has told me, I feel I know you already. Please call me Louise or even Weezie as my friends do."

"Hap's some storyteller, Louise, so I hope he hasn't exaggerated. Let me show you around the castle while we get to know each other."

While the women made their way through the storied fortress now reimagined into the comfortable private residence of the extended Pellegrino family, Hap wandered alone into the library. He was reminded of the first time he had been there more than twenty years ago with Kate. In her typical, proper, southern way, she always found the right hostess gift for every occasion. Although at the time Hap had thought it not terribly appropriate, Kate had given Signora Pellegrino a book about Pittsburgh. To his surprise, he spotted it on a reachable shelf alongside others that based on their titles seemed more appealing. Hap pulled it from the shelf, and finding its binding well worn, he imagined that Kate would have been pleased to know it had seen lots of use. Knowing what was inside, he opened it to find Kate's handwritten inscription, which tugged at his heart. He replaced it quickly when hearing the voices of the women signaling that the tour was concluding.

"Hap, though the formal dinner hour is long past, I have asked the chef to prepare you a simple meal of insalata caprese, pasta Bolognese, and tiramisu. He'll have it delivered to your villa, which is stocked with an assortment of wine, fruit, antipasti, and beverages. Dinner can be at whatever hour you desire. After that, you can settle in for what I imagine will be a good night's rest after such a long journey."

"Oh Contessa, grazie mille."

"Prego, caro amico. Now, why don't you take Dottoressa Porter on a stroll in our special compound while your luggage is moved to the villa."

"Which one?"

"Your favorite of course, the secluded one with the best view and its own infinity pool."

Hap knew the way, and after bidding the contessa a warm "Buona notte," he set out with Weezie so she could see the spectacular vistas from all points of the compass before nightfall.

Along the winding paths through well-manicured shrubbery and flora of all kinds were omnipresent, large, and colorful terra-cotta urns. Hap remembered that they also served the practical purpose of concealing garden hoses curled within for early morning watering by the gardeners. They passed the painstakingly restored ancient stone chapel covered in bougainvillea.

An old-world blacksmith's handiwork was evident in the hand-forged iron straps that had been affixed to its heavy timbered doors to keep them from sagging. Though few worshipped there, given Hap's private worries about Dmitri's next possible move, it was comforting to know such sanctuary was available.

"Oh, Hap, I smell it already. It's heavenly."

"What's that?"

"The lavender."

He played dumb all the while knowing it was her favorite fragrance and would serve as a reliable aphrodisiac for what was ahead. Surrounding their private pool was an uninterrupted, five-foot-tall enclosure of Tuscan lavender. Hap remembered that during the day it attracted swarms of honeybees, which thankfully didn't bother anyone if no one bothered them. He also knew it would be the place for a perfect denouement to their exhausting trip, which he would see to later.

Their villa had once been a stable or a small barn. The living room, kitchen, and master suite were on the ground floor while three additional but on this visit unneeded bedrooms were on the second level. As one would expect, to satisfy the tastes of a twenty-first-century clientele, many windows had been expertly fashioned to fit new cavities cut from the thick stone walls.

Dinner arrived. They were famished, and by candlelight, they devoured most of the delicious owner-inspired meal while Hap told Weezie the story of Lupinari. After unpacking in less than two minutes, Hap stretched out on the bed to watch Weezie do the same, which took far longer. He enjoyed seeing all her things and especially the outfits she would be wearing for the next week. For him, they were like appetizers, and she knew it.

One by one, she unfolded and hung her clothes on silk-padded hangers, but before closeting them, she held each ensemble up for her inspection as if planning on when and where she would wear it. Knowing from experience that some surprises were worth waiting for, Weezie decided that her nighties and undergarments would remain hidden from Hap's eyes in her luggage. Aware of his gaze of contentment but without so much as a glance in his direction, she said, "Hap, you have that look."

"What look?"

"Your game face—the one I could always recognize even in high school. You're looking to get naughty, aren't you?"

"No, I just want to get on with it and do the nasty. How about a little horseplay outside under the stars for a little excitement—poolside and bare ass amid the lavender?"

"As a romantic, you're hopelessly irresistible, Hap, but you really know no bounds."

"Maybe it's the impropriety that I find most exciting."

"Yeah, and maybe you're just a bad boy."

"I thought you fell for only the bad ones, Weeze."

"Was that so apparent?"

"Always. Some might call it a pattern."

"Well, though still very bad, you're different from all the others."

"How so?"

"That would take too long to relate, so how about just getting down to business instead?"

"Shouldn't that be my line?"

"I suppose so, Hap, but now it's time for you to prove yourself worthy of it."

"A vigorous romp is good exercise for the heart in so many ways, but like most things in life, overindulgence can be dangerous. So before any enhanced sex with you, Doctor Porter, you'd better have me sign a liability waiver."

"Oddly enough, I already prepared one, a standard release, but I forgot to bring it, so I'll just have to take my chances that you'll pull through. As for my own safety, and not ever having read the small print on the insurance policy, what if I'm the one not covered for what you have in mind?"

"There's always that, and don't for a minute think I'm not more worried about your stamina, but fear not as I'll be extremely patient in order to bring out all the best in you, capisce?"

"How would you know what's yet hiding within me pleading for an escape?"

"Yankee intuition, my dear."

"So just plain conjecture, right?"

"No; rather, the result of my dedication to a lifetime of field trials. Try thinking of the effort as laboring in the fields and another of my many Pennsylvania Dutch virtues."

"You finally offer something about yourself that I find revelatory, but this is where I get confused about that doctrine. I'd always thought your people led ascetic lives of prayer and abstention."

"We've come a long way from horses and buggies, so I too have tried to keep up by humbly embracing both the ascetic and aesthetic parts of life. I'll leave it to you to guess what category you fall into."

"I'm hoping the latter, or nobody's gonna get lucky tonight. It used to be that only women knew for sure when their men would be getting laid."

"That's a myth, Weeze."

"How can you be so sure?"

"Like I said before, years of clinical trials."

"Are you interested in doing some more research ... like now?"

"Of course. Let's begin. Does a playful, penetrating, and inquisitive tongue still hold any mystery for you?"

"I suppose that's for you to determine."

"Then you'll just have to obey the same instructions printed on all the prescriptions you docs seem to dispense with abandon."

"What would that be?"

"I think the label says take as directed until feeling better."

"Hap, it's obvious you were blessed with an overabundance of charisma but with a big dose of chutzpah in the mix too."

"Don't forget spontaneity, innovation, and improvisation."

"In case you've forgotten, I've always granted you free rein in those areas and courtesies never before extended to anyone. Why don't you close your eyes for a minute while I get ready to prove it? And no peeking."

"I have a feeling this will be an enticement like no other."

Once he complied, Louise kicked off her shoes, dropped her skirt, and removed her blouse, but she decided to leave the rest up to Hap. As if she were not already seductive enough when fully dressed, her intention was to enhance the inducement by revealing some but not all of what she could offer. Upon opening his eyes, what Hap beheld was what he had hoped for as she was clad in nothing beyond pale-blue panties and a matching bra. She knew pink and blue were his favorites, so those were the only colors she had packed. One might suspect blue would have a soothing and cooling effect, but it produced just the opposite, which was her intention.

As she began disrobing him, Hap struggled with her bra. Unfastening them used to be easier and could be done with one hand, but in recent years it had required both to undo them. He figured it was due to an intentional manufacturing defect as opposed to a loss of his manual dexterity. Nevertheless, it provided a newfound appreciation of the merits of a patient, slower-paced seduction.

Their jousting foreplay had accomplished what they had intended it to do, and there was no reason to forestall the outcome. With nothing more to be said, Hap swept her up and over his shoulder and carried his prey off Tarzan-style to the pool. There were no honeybees out at night, and just enough light from a crescent moon for them to keep an eye on what the other was up to. Full-throttled, adventuresome innovation prevailed as the percussive rhythm of their near manic lovemaking accelerated. For the next hour, there were no boundaries as they took turns exercising each other amid the lavender, and then they slipped into the pool to extinguish the lingering flames of their passion.

THE HILLS ARE ALIVE

To RECOVER FROM THE PRIOR EVENING'S SWIM and leftover jet lag, they remained at Lupinari for their first full day. Touring the entire estate on foot was strenuous enough. In preparation for a return to Florence the next day refreshed and sated for a real visit, they retired early but not without a repeat performance of what quickly became a daily amorous ritual by the pool. Despite being exhausted but no doubt enhanced by the lavender, they managed to take the *coda* again and again at increasingly furious cadences before the midnight *sonata* was over. Though unwilling to admit it aloud, both welcomed the change in tempo and privately cherished the *ritardando* that followed their extended *accelerando*.

After an early morning drive to nearby Arezzo, they boarded the train to Florence, where Louise shopped and Hap just watched. It reminded him of previous visits with Kate and the kids in tow. Hap and son Christian had been more than satisfied with seeing the sights and eating all things Italian whereas Kate and Lindsay, who always seemed to have more dollars than sense, shopped till they dropped. Maybe that was Hap's fault for being their complicit central banker all those years, but because it had proven to be a good arrangement then, he expected it to be so this time. After all, it was widely known that men and women had been wired differently by their Creator, and shopping was apparently factory installed by the supreme original equipment manufacturer. Nevertheless, Hap reluctantly did his best not to spoil it though he had long wondered why the shopping app along with a few others could not have been optional.

Thankfully, there was time to visit places they had both been before but never together—the Duomo, the Palazzo Medici, the Ponte Vecchio, and Michelangelo's *David*, or as Christian had once called it, "the big man with the little tinkler." Along the way, he shared some of those fond remembrances with Weezie but was caught off guard by her reaction.

"Hap, you really led such a storied life until I reappeared and screwed things up for you."

"Screwed up? Not by a long shot, and for the record, I think you're better when screwing down."

"Lordy, Hap, can you be serious for once?"

"Not unless I have to be."

"Well how about now? Maybe we could have an impromptu little session right now so I might try to repair what you know is broken inside."

"You might decide it's your rightful obligation to change what's under the hood of this old jalopy."

"And what's wrong with a few updated replacement parts?"

"They might weaken my resistance."

"But make it easier for me to reach the real you."

"Providing you such an entrée would surely turn into something worse."

"Like what?"

"Incessant over-psychoanalyzing of my every motivation."

"Only in retaliation if you ever get fresh with me."

"I might agree to this if we were at Johns Hopkins, but only if there was a couch in your office, and everybody knows all shrinks have one if only to put their patients at ease during the interrogation."

"I'm pretty sure what you have in mind for the couch would be a violation of the doctor-patient relationship."

"But I so like getting fresh. It's my nature, so for now, feel free to explore that side to your heart's content."

"Back home, they'd revoke my license for that no matter how much I might enjoy infringing on the sanctity of my oath. Oh Hap, I can see you won't be serious, so at least be honest."

"Okay."

"Are you feeling insecure in your own skin?"

"See, Weeze? You're already trying way too hard, so time's up for today."

"Hap, you must know that delay is the deadliest form of denial."

"And you're suggesting what? That I'm delusional to believe otherwise?"

"All I'm saying is the recipe used for your DNA has some fundamental design flaws, and I know precisely which ingredients to substitute."

"If ever in doubt, just add sugar, Weeze."

"That's hardly the formulaic strategy needed for you. I know you're not emotionally bankrupt because I've seen plenty of evidence that you have deep feelings, so maybe you're just gun-shy under pressure and use humor as your go-to default mechanism for dealing with vulnerability issues."

"Using humor sure beats doing nothing."

"Then you've turned doing nothing into an art form."

"I do what I can and must with what basic skills and primitive tools the good Lord gave me."

Hap was already hoping the third day would be different if only because there would be fewer places to shop. Women's incessant and often compulsive shopping was an affliction that Hap found inexplicable. Despite his efforts, he'd finally given up trying to curb what he reluctantly accepted as an ingrained habit mothers simply couldn't resist nurturing in their daughters.

Confident as he was that shopping was a gender-specific congenital flaw, Hap was not yet ready to broach such a conversation with Weezie. He also had been wary of ever bringing this notion up with Kate or Lindsay over the years, having enough sense to know there were easier and less painful ways to commit suicide in front of a mixed audience. Men of course had been puzzled about it since the Stone Age and discussed the subject freely and routinely but only when among their own kind. Though missing a shred of evidence to support such a claim, all men knew it to be true.

Because the trip Hap had planned was to be one of relaxing at Lupinari and visiting some of the nearby Tuscan hill towns, he had chosen San Gimignano, Siena, and Montepulciano for their third day. Assisi and his favorite walled town of Lucca were too far for a day trip especially following what had become their inspired, daily, de rigueur romping after dinner and if lucky before breakfast. As both had hoped, the intensity of their passion grew stronger as the days passed even though Hap knew it wasn't going to end well.

The vacation had deliberately been planned to coincide with the annual Palio di Siena festival, which committed another whole day but was scheduled after a down day spent alone with Weezie without leaving their villa. The _palio_ was the oldest horse race in the world. It lasted just over a minute, about half the time of the Kentucky Derby, but like its American counterpart, it was all about pageantry. It was held in Siena's Piazza del Campo, but Hap had never managed to witness it in person, and he believed it would be an exciting experience they could share.

The pomp and festivity surrounding the palio was everything they could have hoped for; the joyful spectators made it even more so. Arm in arm, Hap and Weezie took their time weaving their way through the crowd to enjoy the people and savor snatches of their conversations. Once the shops reopened, Hap did what he knew he had to by visiting one of his favorite hat stores, where he found a wide-brimmed Borsalino fedora to his liking and a straw Panama with a pale-blue floral hatband for Weezie. Borsalino had been making the finest hats since 1857 in northern Italy, and though they could be ordered on the web, Hap never considered a trip there complete unless he returned with one of the country's iconic fedoras. As a cowboy hat was to the wild West, over time, the Borsalino had been the definitive choice of Mafia dons, fashionable Hollywood moguls, and the occasional well-dressed spy.

Because their time in Tuscany would soon end, Hap worried about when and what he should tell Weezie about Cherkov's reemergence and the possible danger it might mean for her. How he would tell her would be equally difficult. He had never been careless with words either spoken or written, and this time, it was important that he chose them very carefully.

WHAT A DAY FOR A DAYDREAM

WHEN OUTSIDE THE BEDROOM, the prim and proper Dr. Porter considered herself private and reserved, but that was wearing off the longer she was with Hap. Given his natural knack for keeping her engaged and entertained, it should not have surprised her, but it did. She was becoming a newer and fresher version of the old Louise, and it somehow suited her more than she could have imagined. Though her work and her daughters had kept her busy, gratified, and fulfilled, for too long, there had been a key part missing. But as in a good novel, Hap had come along and quickly filled the empty places in her heart as she had done to his. There were the requisite reservations. At first, she felt overshadowed by his need to be in charge, but that had been a few years back, soon after they had rediscovered each other. Once Louise understood that dimension and played into it, she was then better equipped to manage him.

Even her first memory of him back in junior high was one of wonder. A shy girl, Louise had been struck by how effortless it had seemed for Hap to be so disarmingly charming at that young age. At the same time, he really put himself out there for what she knew was a heap of unwarranted skepticism by herself and others. In those days, she had thought that Hap was just way too complicated for her, a quiet, restrained, and cerebral gal who was afraid to make a fool of herself, to take on. That would come later, when she allowed herself to be a pushover for men who took advantage of her trust and kind-hearted goodness. If she had only recognized that underneath Hap's adolescent façade was a young man uncommonly serious about what he hoped and desired would be their future. But she hadn't, and that was that.

Only decades later upon learning of his abiding ardor over the years did she realize that he deserved at least equal blame for not sharing those longings with her back then. It may have made all the difference, but maybe not, as they both had needed lots of room and independence to get where they had gotten in life. With much of her past now able to be examined with the benefit and clarity of a rearview mirror, she still had no regrets about any of it. In fact, given the reunion with Hap, she was happy it turned out the way it had.

The trip to Italy was the longest time she had been alone with him at one stretch, and unlike things had been with anyone else beforehand, she was never bored. Even their reflective and silent periods when they were simply reading were exhilarating. If this was the preface of what a full-time arrangement might be like, she knew in her heart it was what she wanted and needed.

Noticing she hadn't turned a page in a while, Hap peered over his reading glasses, smiled, and stared at Louise until finally interrupting her trance.

"Weeze, I can see you're daydreaming."

"How did you know?"

"After years of observation and experience, I can always recognize that faraway look in your eyes."

"And pray tell what might it mean?"

"Simply put, you look very content—in fact, like a living portrait of happiness. Anything I can take credit for?"

"I know you're expecting me to say all of it, so I won't, but I was thinking about our relationship and how it's changed me."

"Relationship? Gosh, I thought we were only star-crossed lovers. If we had a relationship, we'd have one of those joint bank accounts, and that would be a big problem."

"How so?"

"Since you're the one who still works, folks would say that I was a kept man, and I couldn't have that!"

"Oh you! Honestly, I was wondering where you get so much vitality for engaging everyone you meet with disarming humor—waiters, sales clerks, everyone you encounter … Even me."

"Sounds like you're accusing me of being what? Extroverted? Now that's a surprise. I've gotten through life so far thinking I was introverted."

"Hap, I don't think you know the difference."

"Sure I do. Extroverts are energized by social interaction while introverts are enervated by it, so I'm guessing that puts me in the second camp."

"Hap, as your de facto personal therapist, I hesitate to cast a longer shadow on your otherwise insightful self-diagnosis, but you revel in social interaction. I've often wondered what you'd be like if there were just the two of us for company."

"That's easy peasy, Weezie. I'd be horny."

"Apart from that, and try being serious for once."

"I'm always serious, Weeze."

"You don't have a serious bone in your body."

"One immediately comes to mind, and I'm downright disappointed at how quickly you forgot about it."

"You know, Hap, I've diagnosed a lot of head cases, but yours takes the cake."

"Mine should be an open book for an experienced shrink like you who's already familiar with all the symptoms."

"Maybe, but you've got way too much outdated software cranking away up there."

"There's not much room left on that old hard drive. Anyway, I'm not comfortable uploading all that avant-garde scary shit from Silicon Valley … You do know that's in California, don't you?"

"But you like California wines."

"I do, but that's the only export from the Left Coast that I'm comfortable with. Thankfully, when the big earthquake comes, the San Andreas fault will spare the vineyards but will take out all that state's bad parts."

"Lord, give me strength. What I need to know is what a future with you might look like, so let's begin the session with a few questions."

"Okay, but I hope they won't be hard ones."

"Nothing's too hard for you. But enough of that. Look, everyone knows you're a take-charge kind of guy, but how long have you been accustomed to getting your own way?"

"Probably forever. I do so like to prevail."

"Are you a sore loser when you don't?"

"That's never happened."

"Ha! Lose or prevail? In either case, could you remain strong willed without having to go to the mat on every issue when challenged?"

"I may be out of my bailiwick here, but that sounds like a trick question."

"It is, and if you aren't ready to answer, you'd best keep quiet."

"That's usually impossible to do, but I'll take your advice … for now."

"Your silence must mean you have commitment issues we need to work on next time."

"Oh Weeze, anyone would be afraid of being committed. After all, there are lots of weird people locked up in looney bins."

"Always room for one more, Hap."

"There. I knew you'd see it my way."

"You really have mastered the art of evasive segues, but I hope you know this complimentary therapy will be continued."

"I've read that being evasive is an essential quality in a spy, and you know what? I always wanted to be one since seeing the first James Bond movie in junior high. Gosh, I already drink vodka martinis, drive fast cars, and feel right at home in a tuxedo, so maybe I'd be a good spy."

"Ya think? Or perhaps even a spymaster? I'll just add that fantasy to my list for follow-up at your next session."

"Why wait?"

"Okay, let's talk more about the duplicitous part of your life."

"You mean the patriotic side work that doesn't come with a decent pension?"

"Yeah, that stuff, and since it's all behind you now, why not write a book?"

"My target audience would have to be the clerisy and not the clumsy who want only a fast beach read with a superficial story line."

"What's wrong with that? I like books that aren't dumbed down for the masses. Plus, you'd find it impossible to be laconic in speech or the written word."

"It won't sell, but I have a surprise for you, Weeze, and here's the spoiler alert—I already have a finished manuscript cued up and ready for publication."

"Given your impeccable verbal expression, I'm not surprised."

"But it's not about spies."

"What's it called?"

"The working title is *Please Pass the Neuroses*."

"Bet that was easy to write."

"Why?"

"Because you got a second helping at birth."

"But those are legacy neuroses that I'll never work my way through."

"That's a fallacious argument and one I won't accept. All aberrant disorders are rooted in childhood."

"Even a latent proclivity for a good spanking?"

"Especially that."

"What if I'm just eccentric. Would you settle for that?"

"Not without further examination."

"That's what they all say. You shrinks have no real incentive to solve problems because if you did, you'd all be out of work."

"Speaking of problems, Hap, didn't I read somewhere that beyond being the last living icon from the golden age of radio, your mother had a master's in child psychology?"

"Yeah, but she did that later on, in midlife, when I was already in college."

"Why then?"

"Her answer when interviewed by a reporter was that she wanted to figure out where she went wrong with raising her children."

"See? I knew there were others who must have shared my frustration with you."

Louise hadn't expected it would be easy, but she knew being more assertive with Hap had to be part of the equation if this was going to work. Of course, had she known what Hap was doing about Cherkov's threat, she may have understood his reluctance to make promises he might not be able to keep.

WHEN DUTY CALLS

LOUISE KNEW THE MORNING DRILL, and it was no different in Tuscany than it would have been anywhere else. Hap woke at dawn, followed his established regimen of stretches and calisthenics, took a short run, brewed some Italian roast, and then enjoyed some private downtime in deep thought on the patio outside the villa. Since he had once told her that never varying this rigid alchemy had kept him from the nut house, she was loath to disturb him. This time, something was different. Every morning as she watched his solitary routine from the bedroom window, he looked increasingly more distant and troubled. Sometimes, he was so self-absorbed that his coffee got cold.

It was time. That day was their last before returning to their hectic lives. She would confront him but in a roundabout way because her interest was more out of genuine concern than outright curiosity. Wearing nothing beyond her short, sexy nightie, she ventured out onto the patio. Knowing how much Hap liked seeing as much of her legs as possible, when packing sleepwear, she had chosen only the shortest. Even in her bare feet, Hap heard her coming, and without turning startled her with a booming, "Buon' giorno, amore."

"And you too, Romeo. Say, why don't you come back to bed. It's high time you got yourself out of that insular world of yours."

"Sneaking up and snooping around trying to catch me pondering the real meaning of life, huh? You do know I could claim violation of domain as this is my sacred and private time of sanctuary. That said, I do admire your unbridled opportunism when it might involve making more whoopee."

"Hope you're not accusing me of extortion for gratuitous sex. Plus, if you refuse me now, you'll forfeit all such privileges while we're here."

"That's some penalty."

"And it'll be hard on you, Hap."

"It already is."

"Then you'd better make up your mind soon before I rescind the offer."

"Well, okay then, but only because resisting your advances would be overly punitive."

"Ha! Don't forget you're the one who made me so needy."

"How so?"

"When I first noticed your eyes staring at me in the seventh grade, I felt like you'd already undressed me."

"Actually I had, and like now, maybe I was yearning for more."

"If that's so, today's your lucky day, Hap, because I'm gonna ride you like a rented mule."

"I'm pretty sure you'll get your money's worth."

"If not, don't think I won't put the crop to you, Hap."

"You wouldn't dare."

"Don't be too sure. Maybe it's time we up the ante and take it to a new level."

Once in the seclusion of their bedroom, Hap put his arms around her from behind while kissing the nape of her neck and shoulders, an approach that had never failed to make her shudder with excitement. Anticipating his next move, she raised her arms over her head as Hap gently pulled her nightgown up and off, allowing its silkiness to further tease her growing arousal. When the sheer fabric passed over her breasts, she became even warmer to the touch, and her nipples grew taut and more defined.

Trembling with anticipation, she turned to face and embrace him with a passionate kiss while slipping her hands down the back of his running shorts to massage his buttocks. Working her way around to the front, Louise reflexively went for and immediately found what she was seeking and desperately needing. Pleased that the raging fire of his desire required no further stoking, she dropped to her knees for a closer examination. Despite their years of intimacy, Louise still marveled at his equipment. Upon seeing it for the first time a decade before, she wasn't sure she could accommodate him, but she had since found an old-fashioned remedy that had become the final step of their foreplay. She liked to think of it as preparing the way, and preparedness had long been her specialty.

Though in no need of additional coaxing, she gingerly bathed him with her tongue in preparation for the penetrating journey ahead. Louise enjoyed natural moisturizing, but she knew from experience not to linger for fear of bringing him to a conclusion ahead of her own. She continued only long enough to provide Hap the entry and access combination required to ease himself into her midst before the frenzy took over. Her work complete, she rose, smiled, took Hap by the hand, and led him toward the bed to enhance the ecstasy.

Just then, a muffled, unique, but unfamiliar ring tone pealed like a warning bell. Hap knew it was the secondary cell phone from Fort Meade he had hidden in a well-concealed compartment of his luggage. He abruptly dropped Louise's hand and made a beeline to the suitcase saying, "I'm sorry, Weeze, but I have to take this."

"You gotta be kidding, Hap. Now?"

All she heard Hap say when answering was a single word—Cavalier—before he reached the patio to continue the conversation in private. To her further disappointment, there he remained for five or so minutes on the call. She expected that her suspicion about who was on the other end would soon be confirmed. As her body cooled, so did she. Few things about Hap ever rattled her, but that time, she was enraged. In defiant protest, she made the bed and got dressed, knowing it would send Hap the right message when he returned.

When he did so, he remained silent, wearing the look of a petulant child caught in some mischief by a parent.

"Come on, Hap, out with it."

"I've been recalled."

"You mean at Sterling Capital, right?"

Hap bit his tongue, pursed his lips, and offered only a concerned gaze in return.

"Shit! I can't believe it! You're running some kind of operation, aren't you? And right here … on our vacation?"

"C'mon, Weeze. What I do or don't do isn't and shouldn't be everybody's business. In this case, it can't be anybody's. Even yours."

"Hap, just tell me one thing. Why are you so devoted to righting wrong by committing more wrongdoing yourself?"

"It's not a simple answer, and don't ever think it's not burdensome."

"And this is something you can't share with me?"

"Unfortunately not. I knew that would be one of the sacrifices when I signed on for this kind of thing, but it doesn't mean I like it."

"You've always been a man who wore many hats. Maybe too many."

"But this one's my favorite."

"Maybe it's time to mothball that hat, move out of the fast lane, and just live the good life. God knows you're entitled to it after how hard you've worked."

"That was never part of the bargain I made with the Almighty."

"Maybe you should renegotiate that deal. You promised me you were out of the game now."

"They brought me back in, and if the thing I'm working on doesn't go down without a hitch, the good life as we know it may be a memory and the new normal a horrific and repugnant alternative to death itself."

"If it's something of such magnitude, how can you dare shut me out?"

Hap was afraid that coming clean would prove to be another of his mishaps and a costly one at that; even so, after a pensive moment and mincing every word, he relented.

"Weeze, you'd better sit for this, as it may involve you … again."

He began by telling her about the explosion that had leveled his home, the threat from Cherkov, and the initiation of a far-flung investigation into Hap's suspicions about the new activities of her ex-husband. That was all she needed to learn before stopping Hap in midsentence.

"Do you mean Dmitri's alive? How long have you known?"

"Only a couple of weeks. The explosion happened only minutes after you'd left Fox Chapel, and the status of Cherkov wasn't confirmed until I went to Langley and agreed to suit up for this. I've intentionally kept all this from you so we could enjoy our vacation before this turned ugly."

"And has it?"

"Apparently so. The call was about taking the operation to the next level, where I might become involved."

Weezie stared at him in disbelief. This is what she had feared most about Hap—that he might never downshift into the not-so-fast lane and take the off ramp to build some semblance of a normal life with her before the final exit was in sight.

The remainder of their freshly spoiled final day was spent without much conversation; none was needed or possible given the silent undertow. Though Hap wasn't in the habit of keeping his mouth shut, he abided by the old axiom of not speaking unless able to improve on the silence. With a book in hand, Louise sat by the pool lost in thought but never turning a page. Hap took one last hike through the grounds carefully cataloguing every splendid detail in his mind for fear he might never return. For the first time, he felt that life might have been closing in on him, and he couldn't refrain from considering the worst outcome. If he went down, Louise and his children would be lonely but would nonetheless recover.

That night, she mostly just wanted him to hold her. When eventually uniting as one, instead of joy, the intimacies brought only tears to her eyes. Gone was the playful banter that had always been prelude to their lovemaking. Had it happened that morning before the call from Bud, the spontaneity alone would have guaranteed an over-the-top experience and fitting conclusion to the vacation, but it hadn't. Reduced to what seemed more like a dispassionate and perfunctory obligation performed in silence, they knew their customary fervor would never again surpass its former zenith until their lives were rid of Cherkov once and for all.

HOMEWARD BOUND

PACKING UP THEIR THINGS TOOK LESS TIME than the unpacking had, which was to be expected and generally the case for all travelers. Uncharacteristically, especially for them, it also was done in silence. Their predawn departure prevented a proper goodbye to Signora Pellegrino, but Hap had left a personal note for her the night before with the bellman. He had plenty of time for a leisurely drive to Florence before checking in for the return flight, but at times, he couldn't resist racing the Maserati when he had a safe opportunity. Beyond Weezie's pleading with him to slow down from time to time, there was little conversation between them.

Once in flight, there was no reason to lower the barrier between the seats or bother to convert them to reclining berths. It was a day flight and there would be no hanky-panky; besides, neither was in the kind of playful mood required for such frivolity.

"Hap, please know that until yesterday, I was having the time of my life, and before the despair sets in, I want to thank you for such a marvelous vacation."

"This isn't the way it was supposed to end, Weeze, and though it's not the right time now, I had planned to ask you an important question while we were away."

"And I wish you had, because I was prepared to say yes, but not now."

"Is that off the table for good, or can we revisit it once this shit storm with the Russians is over?"

"Let's just let everything play out first before you promise me a life you can't deliver."

For a change, Hap had no response . After staring into her eyes for a moment, he turned away in silence to finish reading the pile of day-old US newspapers provided in first class.

About halfway home and somewhere over the Atlantic, he reclined his seat for a comfortable snooze. When nearly asleep, he felt her hand touch his and softly squeeze it twice. It was her way of saying everything would be all right. Hap knew better; he wasn't willing to make any wagers on the outcome with Cherkov. Nevertheless, he squeezed her back in similar fashion.

WAKE-UP CALL

NO SOONER HAD HAP UNPACKED than he was summoned to Langley. It would be a much longer trip if he were still in Pittsburgh, but it was only a short drive from the CIA safe house in Georgetown that he would start calling home for a while. The opulent townhouse was reserved usually for visits by important foreigners willing to make a trade by spilling the beans and was rarely used by operatives, especially those operating off book. But Bud had wanted Hap close by in case things heated up, which they had during his absence.

After navigating the cumbersome security ordeal, Hap was escorted directly to Bud's office. Sunny's eyes sparkled with affection as she blew him a silent kiss and said, "He's upset and waiting for you."

"Okay, but I'm expecting a real kiss on the way out."

"You can count on that, Cavalier. Now go on in before he goes crazy."

He found Bud in his usual pose poring over multiple files scattered across his oversized and unkempt desk. Bud was like that; he somehow could always find order in chaos. Without looking up or offering any greeting, he said, "Don't let it go to your head, Hap, but your instincts were right about Cherkov."

"Tell me more."

"We've been picking up some isolated traffic about techies being recruited worldwide but never heard from again. Beyond their disappearances, it's becoming a brain drain from the top IT companies and universities that feed them. Given the sheer number, we figure whoever's behind this must have very deep pockets, meaning it's gotta be either the Russians or Chinese."

"But Bud, why limit it to the Communists?"

"Others may share the motivation, but only the Commies have the means to attack us, and given the last election, we're apparently pretty fuckin' vulnerable. In fact, we've been warning Congress and the White House about such an assault for years, but for reasons all too obvious, our sitting president has no interest in mounting an official defense."

"Yeah, what a grand puppeteer he is. With him, there are no longer facts of any kind—just good and bad fiction."

"Anyway, this shit's gotta stop, and though we're not officially sanctioned, I'm going all out on this one with our own assets and hired guns like you. From what we've been able to gather from the families of these displaced kids, their destination was somewhere in the Caribbean, so it could be any one of about seven thousand private islands. We're looking at recent construction sites by satellite and examining cargo records to determine if any unusual shipments of electronic equipment have been shipped there."

"That'll take forever, Bud."

"It'll take what it takes, but there are plenty of resources devoted to uncovering this. We'll have to be patient, and that *we* includes you."

"Never my strong suit, Bud."

"What a shame too. There was a time you could have had any position here, even station chief in Moscow."

"Ha! Now wouldn't that have been a plum assignment."

"Hap, that's the top of the line for an operative with nothing but my job separating a guy like you from becoming the director."

"And how long would I have lasted with the czar and his cronies all gunning for me? Plus, I had, and still have, no interest in moving up the food chain here or anywhere else. Retirement suits me just fine."

"I don't believe that for a minute, Hap. You can't help but carry the generational burden of your father's legacy here. It's in your blood."

"And I don't want any more of it spilled on a sidewalk in a dark alley."

"You might be officially retired, but I know you miss it."

"And why's that?"

"You like living on the edge and following in the footsteps your father prepared for you. One day, you'll be back in full harness … It's your destiny."

"Not until I get some sleep, so if we're done here, I'm heading back to my new swanky and rent-free Georgetown digs for a nap to combat the jet lag."

"Don't get too comfortable there. Your lease is day to day."

Once back in the safe house and because he hadn't done so in Italy, Hap checked his stock portfolios. Curiously, the laptop took far longer to boot up than normal, but when it did, he immediately logged into his elaborate financial platform. Unprepared for what came up, he could only gasp in alarm. His cash reserves had been cleaned out, and his vast public equity holdings were gone. *Impossible!* he thought, but then he remembered Cherkov's promise and realized it was all too true—His supposedly impenetrable network had been compromised and his net worth had all but been eviscerated.

Hap hadn't felt this noxious since the coronavirus pandemic had begun. But that market free fall was different as it had left him plenty of capital to claw his way back from the meltdown. In fact, following his opportunistic instincts, he had timed the market bottom perfectly for an all-out buy-in, and he had emerged a few months later with huge gains and a portfolio larger than he had started with. This time, he had nothing to claw back with, and he couldn't fix anything with an empty toolbox.

He immediately made frantic calls to both his bank and master custodian only to be assured that no protocols had been breached. Electronic trades, presumably authorized by Hap himself, had settled and the proceeds had been wired to various offshore accounts. Anonymity and lack of real human verification were just two of the problems with the new electronic trading platforms. Hap harkened back to the days when business was done the old-fashioned way—with people you had first eyeballed face to face and then came to trust over time.

One of the most trusted was Lorraine, who ran Hap's family office and had access to much of his private affairs excepting his covert side work. But there were abundant clues about that dimension including photos of Hap with several presidents and other world leaders that were framed in his study. She'd always been curious if not suspicious about his connections inside the Beltway, but she had always had the good sense never to voice them.

Because he kept her busy picking up the stray, misshapen pieces from his puzzling life, Lorraine typically took her vacations when Hap was away from home for long stretches. Her refuge that time was Turks and Caicos, where she relished the downtime by mostly just reading trashy novels on the beach awaiting some hunk to buy her a drink. It usually didn't take long as she was a smart, fetching, and saucy redhead, which also meant she could be very selective when choosing partners.

One of the things Hap liked best about Lorraine was her abiding ability to joust even amid panic. Because this was one of those times, he knew it was important for him to engage her in their typical banter to not overly alarm her concerning the catastrophe and especially over an unsecure line. He had to make it convincing without sounding desperate, and he was not surprised when she did not disappoint him.

Lorraine answered Hap's call with her usual, "What's up, boss?"

"Hate to disturb you, but we have an emergency."

"Haven't I heard that a time or two before? In every case so far, it's meant *you* have an emergency."

"This time it's for real, so get your well-tanned sweet ass back here pronto."

"Why Mr. Franklin, how you talk when you're upset, and for the record, we fair-skinned redheads don't tan. We burn."

"Well, I need you and your burned hot cross buns here ASAP."

"You know, Hap, one of these days real soon, I'll be forced to sue you for sexual misconduct."

"No jury in the world would ever convict this innocent face, and you know that. Besides, one look at you and the jealous female jurors would discount your entire testimony."

"But the men would award me a bundle based on my looks alone."

"Not without jury tampering, and even then, I bet they'd be unable to reach a unanimous verdict."

"Actually, I'm at my best facing a well-hung jury."

"No doubt, but enough repartee or I'll be suing you for provocation. Let's get back to my problem, and it's a big one. When can I expect you back?"

"If you had your wits about you instead of wishing you were back in Italy with Dr. Porter, you'd remember that I'm homeward bound tomorrow. By the way, that's by intention, knowing you're always a basket case the first day back and no fun to be around."

"I'll be even less so this time."

"Why?"

"You'll find out. I'd rather not discuss it over the phone. I'm in DC now, but I'll see you bright and early in Pittsburgh the day after tomorrow—not at the house but at the office."

Lorraine was not yet aware that his home was no more, and Hap wanted to keep her in the dark about that for the time being. Fortunately, he maintained an off-premises office in nearby

Aspinwall, where Lorraine usually did her thing. His next call was to Bud on the supposedly encrypted line.

"Good grief, Hap! You left here two hours ago. Did Sunny forget to validate your parking or what?"

"Bud, I've been stripped bare."

"Already? So who's the lucky lady?"

"No, Bud. All my assets have evaporated. We're talking complete financial destruction."

"Damn. You too? Well, I'll add you to the list."

"What list?"

"Seems that a lotta fat cats are getting ripped off. So far, the victims are all CEOs, rich entrepreneurs, the Hollywood famous, and other familiar household names. It's obvious they were not indiscriminately chosen but rather carefully vetted to provide the perpetrator the highest yield. We've wrapped this into a full-blown operation—code name Rasputin."

"So it *is* Cherkov who's doing the plundering? Dammit, Bud! I wish you'd told me."

"Hold on, Hap. Remember you're an outside contractor on this, and we don't know for sure it's him, but it's a good guess he's behind it. And shame on us because he's made all these sophisticated confiscations of capital look like easy pickings."

"This could be much bigger than you think, Bud. The light of day is about to surrender to the darkness, so you need to read me in on every detail from now on."

"That's fair even though you're no longer a sanctioned asset. What else?"

"Look. I'm wiped out. I'll need some dough to get by."

"You really are irrepressible! Like how much?"

"A couple hundred thousand."

"Good God. We're not a federally chartered bank here."

"That'll barely pay my overhead for a few months. It may seem like a big nut, but I'm not asking for a free lunch. If you need collateral, I have some gold bars in my bunker."

"The one in your bombed-out home? Really? Why gold?"

"It's part of my doomsday scenario—the one that few beyond me saw coming. Look, Bud, just have your people get in touch with Lorraine later in the week to set me up with a very secure and anonymous bank account. You do it all the time, and with a lot more for the opposing team, so just think of it as spreading around a little federal financial fertilizer."

Before Bud could disagree, Hap hung up. His worries turned to his son, daughter, and Weezie. Keeping them safe was paramount.

BED CHECK

OTHER LEGACIES NOTWITHSTANDING, the only enduring one that mattered were his son and daughter, through whom he could reach out, touch, and if lucky, influence the future. When Lindsay and Christian were youngsters, Hap had made it a habit to check on them once they were sound asleep. Standing quietly at their doorways, he probably lingered longer than most parents did, perhaps because he had a lot more to be thankful for. Hap loved watching them sleep and even when their slumber turned fitful.

Never forgetting they were blessings from God, he tried to treat them with the reverence they were due. Passing down his storehouse of life's lessons along with what he'd hoped was an abundance of humor had usually worked, though sometimes the humor had backfired. Hap was pleased that both were successful in their own right and had never once asked for anything beyond his love. By inheriting his ambitious drive to succeed, neither one had needed the other thing he had promised, which was enough money to do anything … but not enough to do nothing.

There was plenty of evidence to support the devastating effect of being given everything in life, and Hap had been an eyewitness to that. Early examples began with those childhood friends from affluent places like Fox Chapel, Sewickley, and Shadyside whose names were often followed by Roman numerals. It hadn't been entirely the fault of these kids from privilege, except for eventually perpetuating the practice of never weaning their own offspring from the bosom of swaddling comfort, security, and complacency. Such complicity in the vicious cycle had had its consequences.

Vestiges of the entrepreneurial zeal of their forebearers would diminish with each successive generation until the family wealth was fully dissipated and the birthright extinguished. Hap took great measures to ensure such an outcome would never visit the Franklin family.

Moreover, he had always been careful to infuse his children with only enthusiasm and encouragement but not contaminate their hopes and dreams by sharing any of his nightmares. Despite his anxiety about Operation Rasputin, Hap's calls to them now could not betray his worst fear, which was that he might be putting them in harm's way as he had their mother. He considered how he might warn them without overtly doing so, and he phoned Lindsay first.

"How's my girl?"

"All grown up now, Daddy."

"What? Nobody told me! When did that happen?"

"When you weren't looking."

"Hey, I've always had eyes on you, honey."

"Like when I was little and sometimes faked sleeping while you lovingly gazed at your little princess?"

"And you've kept that little secret from me all these years? For shame."

"Yeah, you're right, so how about my sharing another secret to make up for tricking you?"

"That'd be a good start. Go ahead. Make my day."

"Today we found out some news about your first grandchild."

"And?"

"Soon I'll be able to make another fairy tale come true for you—the one where you used to wake me up with a kiss like Prince Charming did to Sleeping Beauty."

"Are you saying it's a girl?"

"You bet, and we're gonna name her after Mommy."

"Katherine, Katie, or Kate?"

"Probably all three, but not Kitty."

"And you can bet I'll be spoiling her beyond your wildest imagination. You do have room for a pony, right?"

"Hold your horses, Daddy. Maybe you'd best start off with a doll house."

"Fine. After that, I'll move your old racing shell from the barn to Chevy Chase. The Potomac along your property is a better river than the Allegheny for a young girl to row in."

"Easy there, just sit back for once and allow it to happen instead of trying to make it happen."

"That'll be tough for an old bird like me. You might not know it, but I've become rather set in my ways."

"You mean the good old ways with old-fashioned values?"

"Nothing will ever beat them."

"Here's something else to chew on. I've been thinking about what she'll call you, and I think Pap Pap is perfect. After all, it's what I called your father."

"Damn, Lindsay, Pap Pap makes me sound so old."

"Then the orthopedic shoe fits perfectly."

"Hold that tongue, young lady. Remember, I may be arthritic, but you'll always be a whippersnapper wet behind the ears."

"Oh, I'm sorry. Must be another example of my rhetorical carelessness."

"Honey, your pen may be infused with the power of skillful writing, but what spills from your mouth into my ears isn't always as persuasive."

"But Daddy, that's because your verbal dexterity gets in the way of how the world communicates now—It's all abbreviated and doesn't give a hoot about your concern over ongoing degradation of the language."

"Aha, and just further proof that we live in a fallen world."

Having risen through the ranks at an iconic advertising agency, Lindsay was its creative director. Always a gifted and clever writer, she initially made her name as a copywriter penning some of the industry's very best ads. When watching TV, Hap could always identify one of her creations because of its well-chosen words. In a weak moment, she had once confessed to him that the real essence of her job was writing weird stuff that made her laugh. It had made millions of others laugh too, and because her brand of stuff lingered long in consumers' minds, she was much in demand for her irrepressibly impressive wit and compelling vocabulary.

"Lindsay, you know how I feel about language. I abhor what's happened to the spoken and written word. I suppose for the sole sake of economy that your generation no longer has time for any meaningful, expressive dialogue, and that it soon will atrophy into using only acronyms, memes, and emojis in its place."

"Oh Daddy, I love you, and maybe because you're a loquacious dinosaur."

"Did I ever tell you how hard it was growing up in the Jurassic Period?"

"Maybe once or twice, but probably when I wasn't listening. One last thing—I was putting you on about what she'll call you. My first choice was really Poppy, but that makes you sound younger and a lot cooler than you are."

"I love it—Poppy it is, but for the record, I'm cooler than you might imagine."

"Yeah, right. Gotta go, but thanks for the bed check."

"You bet, and hey, remember—"

"I know, Daddy, be vigilant."

"And loosely translated, that really means I love you."

"I've always known there was a beating heart somewhere in you."

Vigilance had always been his closing advice, and that time, he feared the warning was more important than ever.

Hap figured that getting hold of Christian would be harder— It always was. Persuading him to answer his phone usually required an advance text that included the reason for the call. Hap's response was usually a terse warning that Chris would be very sorry if he didn't pick up. They had played that game for years but had never tired of it. When Christian answered, he couldn't help but continue their long-running banter.

"Dad, are you calling me from a blocked landline?"

"How'd you know, Chris?"

"Hate to be the one delivering this spoiler alert, but these days, smartphones display more than just the caller's number."

"My flip phone is already smarter than I am, so why would I ever upgrade? But right you are, I'm on a landline."

"That's just so lame, Dad, not to mention a fairly arcane way of communicating."

"Nothing beats copper wire, son. Plus, Ma Bell invested zillions over the last century stringing it across the country, so I think they rightfully deserve a decent return on that investment."

"Weren't they a monopoly from olden times?"

"Yeah, when monopolies worked and weren't a dirty word. Just so you know, I got one of your brethren—another smart-ass techno wizard, to build me a flip phone with smart guts."

"Congratulations, old timer. Should I send you a long list of apps to download beginning with outdated music?"

"Surely you don't mean the four B's—Bach, Brahms, Beethoven, and the Beatles?"

"No, I was thinking only of homegrown American composers such as Irving Berlin and the Beach Boys."

"Okay, you get extra credit for that one, but remember that music shouldn't be a distraction or provide just background noise for life. You know, Chris, I'd hardly recognize you without those ubiquitous ear buds stuck in your head."

"So you still prefer the archaic way of blasting it surround-style throughout the house?"

"It forces you to really listen and concentrate, but don't you worry—I'll just stumble along in life enjoying the full range of fidelity through only those enormous speakers that vinyl records demand."

"That'd be a problem for me, Dad, as all my music is in the cloud instead of gathering dust at home like yours."

"It wouldn't hurt to get your head out of the clouds and get offa my cloud."

"I love sparring with you, Dad, especially when there's no clear winner. Even at your age, you remain an intellectually formidable opponent."

"That's because I can channel both Peter Pan to remain young and Methuselah for wisdom at the same time."

"Okay, you got me there. Who are they?"

"All right, enough of your crap. I only wanted you to know that I might be off the grid for a while and you shouldn't worry."

"You back to doing that spooky stuff? At your age?"

"I'm not sure what you mean, but I'll be out of the country on business and may not be reachable."

"You would if you had a real phone with an updated SIM card."

Christian wrote sophisticated code for what had once been a promising start-up company that was now the dominant player in next-stage artificial intelligence. Instead of taking much higher-paying offers from the biggest of the global tech firms, Chris had wanted to be on the cutting edge. By getting on that bandwagon at just the right time, he was now one of the world's top coders. It was heady stuff, but Hap couldn't understand much of it. Though well behind the curve and out of his element, he nevertheless tried to learn something from his son every time they spoke. Even as a youngster playing video games, Chris had a vision of how things should and could work instead of how they did. Though he had been unaware of it at the time, that had proven to be a gift that he'd built a career on.

Hap knew he was probably the last cave man on the planet to make handwritten lists while everyone else dictated them into smartphones for instant transcription to an embedded digital notepad. It was not simply about being old school; he had always been able to think better with pen and paper in hand. Even with the kids, he saved up his innermost emotional feelings until Christmas or their birthdays to write them proper letters on engraved Crane stationery using a Mont Blanc fountain pen. It gave him a needed personal connection that he couldn't imagine duplicating with a keyboard. He shouldn't have been surprised when not one but both had asked if he would instead scan and send his letters along for easier retrieval and filing.

He continued with Chris, but he changed the subject from the spooky reference—an issue he hoped wouldn't ever come up again.

"So how far along are your colleagues out there in la la land from making these smart-ass phones safe from those who want to peek inside?"

"It's not my specialty, Dad, but it's virtually impossible to program against corruption of presumably safe data and links of communication. What I'm doing is trying to overcome the ignorance in man by creating enlightened intelligence in machines."

"What if it ends up in the wrong robot's hands and does the bidding of the ignorant?"

"I've been thinking we could reprogram stupid commands that by default would turn into smart ones."

"Like taking a smart bomb sent by some crazy jihadist and turning it around to kill the sender?"

"No. That would take time to ascertain who was right and who was wrong, but maybe something along the lines of jamming the nuclear codes if some idiot in the White House decides to launch a first strike."

"Interesting. So you become judge and jury?"

"Dad, I'm going out on a limb here by betting you have buddies at the Pentagon, and if so, you'd better tell them that war will never be the same from now on. It'll be waged by computers with the best programmers and fought in outer space through the cloud. Since the concept alone is far too unconventional for you old geezers who run things, that brings us right back to what I'm capable of doing."

"And what's that?"

"Something a lot more challenging, like you did at my age by making the world a better and safer place."

"So the Martians will want to move here?"

"Maybe, but being an advanced species, they'd find it intolerable to live next door to you."

"Look, just know that despite your insolence, I love you, so stay safe."

"Awww, Dad, and here I thought you loved me because of my insolence."

"Yeah, there's that too."

"And maybe you're just too diligent a father."

"And you might do well to remember the words of the other Ben Franklin, 'Diligence is the mother of good luck.'"

Still spinning from Christian's veiled reference to the dark side, Hap's head was now focused on what it could have meant. His son had a highly creative mind and always thought outside the box, so it shouldn't have been surprising that he'd figured it out. Then again, maybe he was just fishing. Worse yet, perhaps Christian was more than simply curious about the family business, and like his father and grandfather before him, wanted in. If so, Hap would make sure that never happened. He knew that real warfare such as the one America was on the verge of was a game far different from the virtual ones Christian had waged on his computer as a teenager. Though Hap had deftly dodged the question that time, he feared it might come up again and had to prepare for it.

Actually, it didn't trouble Hap that his son and daughter considered him a living anachronism with throwback idiosyncrasies. They never tired of repeating the stories as evidence to prove their claims. All were legendary; some were apocryphal. Besides routinely turning off unnecessary lights as he moved through the house, it was second nature for him to adjust the thermostat down in winter and up in summer. They never let him forget that he had absentmindedly turned off the oven on Thanksgiving turkeys two years in a row. Though Kate had tried to change that behavior by affixing colorful post-it notes that read Don't Touch, the kids had taken turns checking the oven ever since.

That was a time when the unwritten but cardinal rule among spies was that family members were off limits. For men of that era including Hap and Dmitri, it was like a code of honor among thieves and never violated. Sometimes, spies got whacked by the other side; it was, after all, just business, and, well, business was business. Hap had done the right thing by Dmitri Cherkov's daughter by providing her sanctuary under witness protection in the United States. But that didn't assure him that the bastard would follow the same rules by refraining from terrorizing Hap's son and daughter.

NOW YOU SEE IT, NOW YOU DON'T

H AP HAD TO GIVE CHERKOV DUE CREDIT. From what he had learned from Bud, the slew of cyberthefts from America's elite was not limited to pilfering their domestic bank and brokerage accounts denominated in dollars but also those in a variety of online currencies including bitcoin. Cryptocurrency networks lacked uniform regulation, and transactions were difficult to track. Blockchain settlements through a growing number of these virtual assets circumvented normal scrutiny and avoided possible sanction. Most believed that tax evasion and anonymity were the principal drivers of such activity.

Drawn more by curiosity, Hap had dabbled in the crypto market when bartering for big-ticket goods and services, but he kept his financial exposure limited to what he could afford to lose. Though his initial interest in seeing how it worked was a practical one, after understanding the attraction and its applicability to his own world, he had reverted to more-traditional means of accepting and making payments.

If the source of the pirating was in the Caribbean, cleaning Hap out was probably the first catch of the day for Cherkov but likely only a minor distracted effort in the Russian's sport fishing for big game. Though utterly devastating to Hap, the personal take from him would pale in comparison to Cherkov's catch from others. Based on his own study of the vulnerabilities in cyber-criminal activity, Hap knew that reeling in the biggest of trophies involved no more work than netting the smallfry.

The total take could be staggering, and it would happen quickly. Even after passing along the czar's enormous cut,

Cherkov could easily become the world's richest tycoon and thus that much more difficult to bring down. As for the czar, his personal wealth was already sagging under its own weight. Russian law prohibited the negotiation of all transactions other than those settled in rubles, but such a prohibition didn't apply to the czar. Much like the current American president, who invoked executive privilege daily, he considered himself above his own sovereign law. The Russian president's graft was skimmed from things both legal and illegal by readily accepting tribute in all forms. He preferred euros and greenbacks to his own currency, and he was all too happy to begin adding cryptocurrencies as a means of payment for the obvious reasons.

The only risk was keeping Cherkov under a heavy thumb. The czar had already seen his primary oligarch derail once before, and he knew it was the result of a dangerous combination of pride and an overreaching grasp for power. Though shrewd, the czar wasn't a learned man and hadn't read Shakespeare, but he understood well those who suffered from overweening pride. And like Macbeth, he knew how to deal with them.

In contrast, the predicament Bud faced was that he hadn't yet decided how he'd deal with Cherkov especially since the operation was no longer off book. As expected, Hap believed there was just one solution— the single sanction, and he begged to personally administer it.

When the CIA went in search of someone, the target was assigned one of three options: alive at all costs, dead or alive, or the single sanction. The latter meant a confirmed company kill followed by cremation to ensure deniability. Incineration was final and left no trace, which was a must in Cherkov's case. Best of all, there was no reporting to a congressional subcommittee when such a wretched character was tagged with the single sanction. Though customary to get the president's prior approval for such a hit, it was not always sought, and in those cases, there would be no incriminating paper trail.

Inflicting torture let alone the elimination of enemy combatants had become an increasingly problematic issue. If put to a vote, its vocal detractors would surely outweigh the silent supporters, but that wasn't the way things were done in America. The inspired opposition had attracted legions of pro bono lawyers who were already busy seeking legislative elevation of murder to include assassination by drone. To those in the intelligence business, drone kills seemed like nothing more than any other legitimate tool of military conflict, and more important, a way to keep the troops safe from having to engage in conventional combat.

For those reasons, but only after much anguish, Bud concluded that he could not order an assassination for fear of not only a rebuke but also a very harsh one from the director and those further up the chain of command. As well, Langley could ill afford the public scandal a leak would cause in the new environment of semitransparency. Reluctantly, he insisted that Cherkov be taken alive at all costs. Bud expected Hap to protest, but he knew he would follow orders. Though knowing he couldn't guarantee it, he promised Hap that Cherkov's capture would not end in a catch-and-release scenario like the last time.

PART V:
Allegro

THE BUTCHER OF BRUSSELS

THE INTERNATIONAL SYMPOSIUM IN BRUSSELS had been in the planning for three years, and Louise was a featured speaker. She was fast becoming the world's leading expert on stress disorders, so appearing on such a platform would go far in strengthening that reputation. Weezie was excited about the opportunity and had looked forward to it. Hap, however, was not and did not. Given what had happened to his home and the extent he suspected Cherkov was willing to go to destroy him, he was more than apprehensive about Weezie making the trip alone. At the same time, he also knew that accompanying her might only put her in greater danger.

Unfortunately, and despite Hap's imploring, Bud didn't have the budget to send a security detail to watch her back. Reluctantly, she had promised to pack the special backup cell phone that Hap had procured from the techies at Langley. It bore no brand, didn't take photos, and couldn't synch with social media, but it did a whole lot more than just making and receiving calls. Beyond that, she would be on her own.

Hap had insisted she use a private car service instead of cabs at all times especially to and from the airport. Taking it a step further, he had even arranged for the same one the CIA used in Brussels, but he could not have imagined that the armed driver wouldn't make it for his first pickup to meet Louise's inbound flight. Though still warm, the chauffeur's body was already in a cold, shallow grave. His liveried imposter, holding a sign bearing Dr. Porter's name, was waiting at the baggage carousel when

Louise arrived. He greeted her in perfect English and without a trace of his native Russian.

When Louise climbed into the shiny black Mercedes, she didn't immediately notice that the windows were tinted and there was another passenger on board. When she did, it was too late. The man quickly immobilized her while covering her mouth and nose with a handkerchief soaked in a powerful sedative. Louise quickly slipped into unconsciousness before even grasping what had just happened.

The drug wore off. She found herself alone on a cot in a cold, Spartan cell that reeked of urine. It was certainly not her intended destination, which had been the Hotel Indigo. She had no idea how much time had passed since her captivity began or if she was in Brussels or somewhere else. Because of its clammy dampness and the fungi growing along the mortar joints of the stone walls, she sensed her accommodations were underground.

It was clear her luggage had been ransacked; beyond the cell phones, all her jewelry and most of her underwear were missing and no doubt already divvied up among her jailors as souvenirs. They had been under strict orders that she was not to be abused in any way, and thankfully, no harm had come to her so far. That would be saved for later. It was there she would wait until the first of her procedures could be scheduled.

The world's second-best reconstructive plastic surgeon practiced in Brussels, but only the world's most celebrated criminals knew that and how to find him. The difference between him and others around the world who resculpted faces for a handsome living was the outcome. There was a reason he had been tagged the Brussels Butcher. For the right kind of money, he was willing to forsake all traces of humanity and compassion by hastening along the atrophy of natural beauty to a horrendous ending. Permanent disfigurement was his specialty, and that was precisely what Dmitri Cherkov had in mind for Louise Porter, MD.

It could not have been more convenient for Cherkov to put the plan in motion. It was nearly uncanny that Louise had brought herself to the doorstep of the butcher himself. Brussels was known around the world for a lot of things, but not for a series of operations that would make a face like Weezie's one that every onlooker would turn away from in horror. Hideous to look upon and repulsive to touch would be her fate. Cherkov basked in the satisfaction that even Hap would be unable to gaze at her without feeling pity that would also fuel a seething rage. Rearranging his former wife's face into something forever gruesome would be his lasting revenge on her and Hap. His creation would be a hybrid creature with a human and beast-like appearance. She would be a jarring spectacle to behold, like a reverse Pygmalion effect gone bad.

Beyond the horrific result, he could make it an agonizing recovery for the patient too, particularly if the postsurgical pain killers were withdrawn prematurely. Cherkov, who had a voracious, feral appetite for torture, viewed it as no more than an appropriate penalty for her choice of Hap over him. It was time for him to unveil himself, and he would enjoy it.

Louise's cell was unlocked, and two burly men in commando attire appeared. Carrying an overstuffed leather upholstered wing chair, they placed it in the corner and resumed their posts flanking the open door. Suddenly, a far-better dressed man entered and took his time settling into the chair before addressing the bewildered Louise.

"So Mrs. Cherkov, how's my beloved wife?"

The astonishment on her face was what he had hoped to see, but that would be only the first of many rewards he had come to claim in Brussels. His real satisfaction would come later.

"Dmitri, is that you? I hardly recognize you."

"I've had some expensive external repairs made, but I remain the same inside. Besides, I'll always be forever yours."

"I thought you were dead! You should know that I'm now officially your widow."

"How quickly you forgot your solemn vow—till death do us part. I'm very much alive and have no intention of dying. How about you?"

"Why am I here? What's your intention?"

"I'm using you as bait to bring some unimaginable pain and grief to your friend Hap Franklin."

"Why?"

"He took what was mine, including you, and must be severely punished for such a transgression."

"You never wanted me. You only used me."

"But that's why I wanted you. Unfortunately, in my new life, I have no further need for you. Don't worry. Your life will be spared, and you'll be getting a new face as well, but not one you'll like."

"Where's Hap? Do you have him?"

"Not yet, but I soon will, and that's the last question you're entitled to for now."

Cherkov stood, flashed Louise the nauseating, smirky grin she had seen before, and then strode out as the guards removed his chair before locking her up.

Both of Weezie's cell phones had been debugged and their locations camouflaged by a Russian IT wizard before being placed in a lead-lined briefcase. Once they were again operable, the phones were delivered directly to Cherkov, who would be the only one answering the call he knew would be coming. It would be from Hap Franklin, and it didn't take long.

A CALL TO ARMS

T FIRST, ALL HAP KNEW WAS THAT WEEZIE had fallen off the grid. She had never checked into her hotel, and she was not answering either of her phones. It was only when he learned from Bud that her driver was missing that Hap suspected Cherkov was somehow in the mix. Despite her insistence, his letting her travel unescorted had been a foolish mistake. Whenever Hap had given in to anything that defied his instincts, bad things usually happened, and he feared that this was no exception. For most of his life, he had managed risk, but then, when it counted most, he feared that his winning streak might have ended. After repeated attempts, her phone was answered but not by her.

"Hello, Franklin. I knew you wouldn't give up."

"What have you done with her?"

"Nothing yet, but that could change if you don't do as you're told."

"Where is she?"

"Safe with me in a little-known hotel of horror where you will join us. It's in Brussels, and you'd better come alone or it will be lights out for the good doctor."

"How will I find you?"

"I'll find you once you're here. When we've confirmed you're alone, you'll be given instructions by phone. The call will be from this number, which by the way, cannot be traced, so don't bother trying."

The line went dead, and Hap considered what his next move should be. He had to keep Bud in the loop, but he couldn't jeopardize Weezie's safety by telling him everything. This time, he would not waver from his gut feeling, which was that he needed to follow Cherkov's orders no matter that his own life would then be on the line. All too familiar with the anomaly of Cherkov's behavior, Hap knew it would escalate and feared it could become even more deviant with Weezie as his hostage. After rehearsing it in his mind, he called Bud.

"It's time to kick Operation Rasputin into high gear, Bud."

"What's that mean, Hap?"

"Cherkov's in Brussels, where he has Weezie imprisoned, but the specific location was not revealed."

"How do you know this?"

"He answered Weezie's cell phone and issued me a very personal invitation to join him, so I need you to put a crack team together for backup."

"So you're giving me orders now?"

"Look Bud, I need to run this my own way with no second-guessing, and we need to move fast."

"Okay, I'll put this together pronto. You just take it easy and bank a little shut-eye before departure. You're gonna need it."

It was hardly just happenstance that Cherkov was there when Weezie needed Hap the most. Though Brussels was not the easiest place to carry out an abduction, it would have been no more difficult than anywhere else in the world for a man with the unlimited global resources Cherkov had. He could make her disappear without a trace, or worse, personally make sure she experienced some of the ruthless and zealous wrath he was assuredly saving for Hap. If his intention was to cripple Hap emotionally forever, depriving him of Weezie would be the way.

As when Kate was killed, Hap dreaded this would be like that again. Luckily, Weezie had come along just in time to fill the void left in his heart by the loss of Kate. Eventually, Hap hoped he would be able to check all the old, unneeded baggage and move on, but he knew that wouldn't be possible until all unfinished business was settled, and Cherkov headed that list.

Weezie was indeed the complete package, and when the gift box was removed, inside was a real gem that was brilliantly cut and multifaceted. Their mutual adoration had proven steadfast over time, and above all, Hap now knew she completed him in every way. Being deprived of her fervent love was not something he could endure or allow.

BIRDS OF A FEATHER

AP'S FIRST STOP WAS FORT MEADE to pick up some toys, many of which required special instruction and demonstration. The new tools of tradecraft were far more advanced than those he had available when he had been in service to the flag, but he didn't think they'd be that much help for his mission. All he wanted was a few reliable weapons and communications gear, but he was forced to take it all.

Another reason Bud made Hap go to Fort Meade was to be chipped so that his whereabouts could be pinpointed at any time. Not much larger than a pinhead, the tracking device was easily implanted between two of his toes without any preparation. The post-procedure dressing was no more than a drop of skin glue and a small Band-Aid that would be removed the next day leaving no trace of the incision.

Bud had insisted on veiled secrecy with all things related to Operation Rasputin, but Hap preferred calling the target by his given name. If nothing more, Cherkov seemed a suitable aptronym for such a vile prick. Hap also had his own way of preparing for battle. He would find a quiet place, close his eyes to better focus, and then channel the enemy to feel his evil before making his next move. That time, he helped the exercise along by sipping some vodka, but certainly not Russian vodka.

Before the team's departure for Brussels, and as was the case with all missions under his direct auspices, Bud insisted on a final strategy meeting. That time, Bud met Hap at the Georgetown safehouse, arriving on foot and incognito. Hap had to stifle a laugh when answering the door until Bud was well inside and out of earshot of any passersby.

"Good God, Bud, you couldn't fool anybody in that getup. That hobo of an outfit looks so out of place on you and the fake mustache doesn't even match your hair color."

"I don't get to do this kind of thing much anymore and couldn't resist giving it a try myself."

"Well, believe me on this—You should never do your own makeup again."

Once both had a drink in hand and were seated, Hap just stared in anticipation, waiting for Bud to tell him something he didn't already know.

"Hap, you're a rare bird in this business."

"What you really mean is I don't take orders or criticism."

"There's that too, but let's face it, you've managed to pull some outrageous stunts and get away with them. But your guardian angel, or Lady Luck as you once called her, is getting a bit long in the tooth."

"I know it's been a few years since I've had field duty, but things worked out just fine the last time I was on an assignment like this."

"How well I remember. You were the only one who walked away. All the others were carried away in body bags."

"Rightly or wrongly, Bud, fear of failure has never been a deterrent."

"Just promise me you won't be foolish enough to run amok and jeopardize this thing. I won't stand for any cowboying. What I really need are your instincts and good intel, not improvisational moves that will get you and the doc killed."

"I suppose that's as good a reason as any, but there's one thing I want when this is over—That is, if I survive."

"The suspense is killing me."

"I want to see the unredacted file on my father."

"For Christ's sake, Hap, not that again! I made that request for you years ago right after you learned he had been one of us. As you already know, it was summarily denied. Anyway, that was light-years ago. He'd been recruited by Bill Donovan himself and was a holdover from the OSS after the war ended. It's ancient history, so just leave it alone."

"Until just now, I didn't even know that much, so you must have seen the file."

"Maybe, but if so, that would have been during your recruitment years ago."

"You don't forget anything, Bud, and besides, I'm less curious about what capers he was involved in than what motivated him to join the dark side."

"Dark side my ass, Hap. We're all patriots here. What I do recall from boning up on your dad is that the two of you are birds of a feather and both strange birds at that."

"That alone gives me comfort, but not closure. Now that you've established that there is, or at least once was, a file, I'll have something to look forward to when this thing is over. Think of it as an incentive for me to keep myself in line until then."

Even though it may not have been Hap's father's conscious intention, it was obvious that he had prepared the way for Hap all along. After all, fathers couldn't help but mold their sons in their self-image. Although reading his father's file might provide some clues as to what had drawn him to a covert second life in espionage, Hap didn't expect to find proof of the underlying motivation. As for solving other issues that still separated them long after his father's death, Hap knew he might never discover the conclusive evidence he longed for.

"How about another drink, Bud? I know this place is crawling with bugs, but I'm equally sure you had the foresight to shut them all off for your visit."

"How right you are, as always. I can't have the boys in surveillance recording me drinking on the job. Plus, this gives us one of those rare opportunities to talk off the record."

"Just like the folks at Terminix, and thanks to all that training at the Farm, I found most of the bugs and at least one of the cameras when I moved in."

"So I heard; in fact, they sent me a screenshot of you giving the camera the finger."

"I find myself flashing the bird more and more as I get older. Condescension comes naturally with aging. But back to this fancy safe house ... Despite the cost to the American taxpayers, it's such a shame that only foreign diplomats and the occasional operative get to use it. I mean, really, Bud? Designer toiletries, complimentary terry cloth bathrobes, and silk sheets?"

"Don't forget the bar full of top-shelf booze and the larder of fresh food."

"Spoiler alert, Bud. I'll be taking all the French-milled soap, shampoo, and other sundries with me when checking out. Remember that old Pennsylvania Dutch saying, waste not, want not. In fact, I could use the bathrobes too as mine weren't covered under my homeowner's policy when the house was leveled. All they lack are my monograms hand-embroidered just above the CIA logo."

"You really are an enigma, Hap, or at the very least a multidimensional contradiction in so many ways."

"How so?"

"Though I'm not old enough to be your father, I've always thought of you as a son, so bear with me. I wouldn't say you're miserly, but you do enjoy pinching pennies, so let's call you ... What? Parsimonious?"

"I suppose that tag works, Bud, but it's more about despising waste of any kind. I've been around plenty of profligate spendthrifts, and I can't help but feel all that extravagance could instead be saved for something better like feeding the hungry and providing shelter for the homeless."

"Hap, I'm in awe of some of the philanthropic things you do behind closed doors, which is often hard to reconcile with your overriding focus on thrift."

"Oh don't get all weepy on me, Bud. After all, there's another dimension. Without many deductions beyond charitable giving left in the tax code, I'd sooner give it away instead of paying taxes to support things like this townhouse of yours."

"I'd forgotten your practical side."

Absent the usual threat of being snooped on, their conversation turned to the bigger picture. Even if played out publicly, they both knew this operation concerning Cherkov and the Russians wasn't the real threat to the homeland. Rather, as most in the intelligence communities were well aware, the United States was China's primary impediment to global supremacy and world domination. The leaders of the Chinese Communist Party, had put their plan in motion long ago through predatory economic infiltration while promoting subversion of all things American.

As Hap had learned from his son, Chris, war ultimately would be waged far from sight in a new domain. The next frontier was not on land or sea but in space, where sophisticated efforts of weaponization were already taking place. Settling conflict there would not harm the earth's atmosphere and perhaps be concluded without a single casualty. Knocking out an enemy's military and commercial satellites that controlled communication and other critical things like GPS guidance systems would put an end to conventional battle.

Before calling it a night, Hap and Bud agreed that there was only so much they could do, but they were nevertheless determined to do what they could. Getting China to back off would involve more than a scuffle. Playing fisticuffs with so powerful a dragon was a daunting challenge, but if all the stars were aligned, it was yet possible to turn things around. It would require cooperation with the media, which could help arouse the public imagination to include a rightful focus on what China was really after.

A-HUNTING WE WILL GO

HIS GO BAGS WERE LOADED FOR BEAR, and in this case, *the* bear. The driver had been early and was awaiting Hap's signal that he was locked, loaded, and ready to roll. As usual, Hap also was prepared well ahead of time, but due to his proclivity for precision in all matters, he didn't flick the vestibule lights on and off until precisely the agreed-upon time. After carefully surveilling the street, the driver, clad in a nondescript black suit and wearing an earpiece, approached the door to help Hap with his baggage. As was his nature, Hap refused the assistance having already slung his two duffle bags over his shoulders like any other beast of burden.

Not surprisingly, the vehicle was also black—an SUV with tinted windows and probably bulletproof glass. A comfortable Lincoln Town Car would have been more to his liking, but the seventh floor was hell-bent on doing things the same way their operatives were depicted on TV and in the movies. It seemed to Hap that traveling in this fashion did nothing more than broadcast to any onlookers that something spooky was going down. For an agency whose supposed specialty was stealth, the brass had gotten their dress codes and modes of transportation all wrong.

The short trip to Maryland's sprawling Andrews Air Force Base was tolerable because for the most part, the driver kept quiet during the late-evening ride. Beyond sharing its cost among those who used it, Hap never understood why it had been renamed Joint Base Andrews. Legitimate flights like the one he was about to board made sense, but some others like those taking members of Congress on foreign vacations disguised as fact-finding missions didn't. The most egregious flights involved ferrying the president's entourage on Air Force One to and from his all-too-frequent rallies, and they seemed no more than an extravagant taxpayer rip-off. One of the few icons on Hap's phone was the national debt clock, which was running faster every day trying to keep up with the bloated federal deficit.

Once cleared to enter the tarmac directly, the SUV was escorted by two other vehicles to the overnight bird that would ferry Hap nonstop to Belgium's Chièvres Air Base. He immediately recognized it as a C-37A, which was military speak for what in civilian life would otherwise be a Gulfstream V. Despite its lofty sticker price, but particularly on a long haul, Hap knew the G-Five would provide far more comfort and luxury than Sterling Capital's Citation he was accustomed to flying. Notwithstanding the lack of any distinguishable outward markings, it also would be comparable to other aircraft that routinely delivered foreign diplomats to Chièvres, which was home base for NATO and SHAPE—the Supreme Headquarters of Allied Powers in Europe.

Before Hap could object, his bags were removed by the driver and handed off to another man in black. The two could have passed for twins. Instead of being loaded into the plane's cargo belly, both bags were taken aboard and stowed in the passenger compartment. Soldiers of all stripes needed to have their toys at the ready if trouble erupted, and Hap was no different.

He followed the man up the airstairs and stepped into the cabin only to see a dozen others seated and ready for departure. They too were all in black, but theirs was casual wear of identical turtlenecks, stretch pants, and high-end sneakers. From their collective demeanor, they looked like serious ninja-type warriors indeed capable of and eager to get in harm's way if provoked or ordered. They looked the part of battle-hardened combatants, and since this was a black-bag job, they were likely a combination of retired army Special Forces and navy SEALs—decorated veterans now working for outside contractors. Once prey themselves, they had become accomplished hunters, and they never wasted any effort discriminating between the good and bad targets they were assigned.

"Gentlemen, now that your curiosity has been satisfied and hasn't yet killed the cat, I bet you were expecting a younger version of the guy you've been charged with keeping alive, right?"

Though no one answered, Hap's comment was just what was needed to break the silence and set them at ease. He also knew they yearned for more from him before passing judgment.

"You know, you guys look scary enough without wearing all black. Who dressed you? Certainly not your mothers … Probably some half-assed costume director from Twentieth Century Fox."

All smiled, and some laughed. They had known only the legend, but at that point, they had gotten a good first taste of the man, and they liked him. Selfishly, Hap knew the importance and personal benefit of endearing himself to a team that might be the only thing separating him from Cherkov's wrathful vengeance. These men were mercenaries, no more than hired guns on their way to just another day at the office. Unlike Hap, they had no personal skin in the game, but by the time they arrived in Belgium, he wanted to make damn sure they did.

Since Hap was going in as a lone wolf, there was no need to introduce him to the other players before game time. Instead, and as Bud had intended, the roughly eight-hour flight would give them plenty of time and ample opportunity to get acquainted. Besides, the ninjas would be remaining in the background unless backup was demanded. Once on the ground in Chièvres, they would disperse and take separate ground transportation to the target site in Brussels. Trouble was, Langley hadn't yet determined its precise location. Of course, they wouldn't and couldn't know that without Hap's alerting them once he himself knew, and there was always a chance that that might not be possible.

In retirement, Hap had tried to be invisible to the CIA, and he imagined it would be no different from his successful separation from Sterling Capital. Perhaps it would have been had Cherkov been put down when they had him the first time. In Hap's view, it was therefore Langley's fault for bringing him back to clean up matters after they had dropped the ball by releasing Cherkov. Langley was equally to blame for not discovering what the Russian oligarch had been up to since.

Though most of the CIA's twenty thousand employees spent their time gathering and parsing a plethora of information, little of it was valuable or actionable. Having sat in one of those chairs, Hap understood that the interception of intel was easy while making sense of it wasn't. Things were never as they appeared, so it took brains and imagination to make something relevant out of what might have appeared useless.

Nothing in the world was sacred from the prying electronic eyes and ears of the office. With the advancements in technology, playing peekaboo with the enemy was more like an exciting kids' game. That was just one reason Hap believed that only boots on the ground could gauge the level of evil lurking in the hearts of the enemy. Nevertheless, whoever had been charged with keeping a watchful eye on Cherkov must have been fast asleep at the switch.

As always, it was the role of the agency's few remaining field operatives to finish up what would be papered over if it didn't go well. Bud expected Operation Rasputin would go as planned or had at least tried to fake that attitude when paying Hap that last-minute visit before departure. Hap recalled their final words, wishing he hadn't been so flippant in response to Bud's sincerity.

"Good luck, Hap, and try to remember that your role in this should be nothing more than a cakewalk, so put your ballet slippers back on and get to work. And please, just sit back, get out of the way, and let the other guys do their thing."

"Bud, it's okay if you want to be my surrogate father, but now you're sounding like an overly protective mother sending her son off to summer camp for the first time."

Hap didn't blame Bud for trying to diminish the danger; after all, that was his role as coach. Thanks to Hollywood, there would always be those who glamorized the work done by Hap and other covert agents, but those in the know knew it was a tough, gritty business fraught with peril at every turn. Given what Hap knew about Cherkov, he expected nothing less, and privately, so did Bud.

INQUISITION

ASSISTED BY MI6 AND THE SPY SERVICES from a few other trusted allies, the CIA had identified the coordinates of several possible hideouts for Cherkov to keep Weezie under wraps in. It was decided that Hap and his team would split up to evaluate all of them but only in reconnaissance mode. Ever the renegade, Hap already knew the general location from the second call from Cherkov, but he hadn't conveyed that to Bud. He knew the only way this would work out was to follow Cherkov's instructions, which were that he come alone and unarmed. For that reason, he assigned himself to surveil the neighborhood where Cherkov had told him to visit and stroll along the sidewalks until summoned. Neither he nor the spooks at Langley were aware that it was an area where an aging relic had been dormant and decaying for seventy years. The secret underground stronghold, a bunker built during the war in which the Nazis held and interrogated spies, would serve as an ideal location for what Cherkov had in mind. No one could have imagined that it was there that Hap would keep his appointment with Cherkov.

When bad things had happened to Hap, they had usually come as complete surprises. Though this time would not be one of them, he knew that if and when tapped on the shoulder from behind, he'd better be prepared to face danger. No matter how foreboding it might seem, when the time came, he wasn't planning to go down without a fight.

After an hour's aimless walk and all the while suspecting he was under surveillance, Hap answered the third and final call from Weezie's cell phone, listened to his instructions, and confirmed them. In full compliance, he presented himself at the door of a shop selling Belgian lace. The sign said it was temporarily closed for renovation, but Hap knew differently. He pressed the doorbell three times. He was greeted by two burly men in black with holstered Makarovs, which he recognized as formerly the preferred sidearm used by the old KGB. Black was the universal dress code color for spies, mercenaries, hit men, and undertakers, and Hap thought these two looked like they could have passed for any or all four of those varieties.

Without a word spoken, the two flanked Hap, blindfolded him, and strong-armed him to a back stairway that led to the basement. Once there, they descended yet another staircase that began under a trapdoor hidden in the floor. Knowing that he had to conserve his strength for what was assuredly ahead, Hap didn't resist, but he also didn't make it easy on his escorts. By dragging his feet, they were forced to lift and carry him. When finally placed into a chair, he felt the needle and then no more.

When he came to, Hap was surprised to find himself in an uncontrollable shiver. Once fully conscious, he opened his eyes and slowly lifted his drooping head from his bare chest to discover why it was so cold. For the first time in a long time, he was alarmed and frightened. He had been stripped naked and strapped to an oversized steel chair; his arms and legs were bound by iron manacles that had been welded to a chair permanently set in a concrete platform a few feet above the floor. The chilly clamminess of the place meant he was probably underground though he had no immediate recall of how he had gotten there.

As Hap's eyes adjusted to the dim light, the three men who sat before him came into focus. One of them rose and approached Hap but warily kept his distance while circling the contraption that held him captive. Seeing that all was secure, the better-dressed man resumed his seat in the comfy armchair positioned between two tattered ones occupied by equally emotionless yet menacing men who appeared to be his bodyguards. On the table before them were three glasses, some ice, and several unopened, opened, and spent bottles of vodka. At first, the scene looked like a courtroom setting, but Hap knew it was an inquisition.

"Well, Franklin, we meet again, but this time no longer as strangers."

Newly chiseled features had improved his face, and tinted contact lenses had altered the true color of his eyes, but the indelible stamp of systemic evil could not be erased. The voice, even absent his onetime Russian accent, was unmistakable. Without any doubt, Hap now knew he beheld a new and improved Dmitri Cherkov. Hap stared in disbelief and could only speculate about how long, extensive, and expensive the do-over must have been. Finally, he responded.

"Nice place you've got here for a conclave, and yes, Cherkov, some might say we're strangers no more."

"So Franklin, you recognize me."

"Evil is impossible to disguise."

"I don't imagine you've ever seen any of my handiwork up close, so let's begin with a question. Which would you rather lose—your hearing, your eyesight, or your voice?"

"That's a tough choice, but didn't you promise to take everything from me?"

"As you'll soon learn, I'm far from done taking everything that is yours. And since you don't want any say in your own devastation, I'll make the decisions for you. We'll spare only your sight, which will give you the opportunity to forever look at what I have planned for Louise. But I promise that the result will make you regret having working eyeballs."

"Where is she?"

"Nearby and awaiting what let's call elective surgery. For now, think of it only as a highly creative procedure. You'll eventually be able to see her, and when you do, I too will be there if only to witness the shock and horror on your face."

"Leave her out of this, Cherkov. You got me to do with what you want."

"But torturing you will involve destroying her."

"Look, I'm begging you for an act of clemency for Louise. You owe me that. After all, I once granted you life over death."

"That's not in the cards, Franklin. You should have killed me in Saint Petersburg when you had the chance because you'll never have another. You were weak and couldn't pull the trigger. We would never tolerate such compassion in the KGB, FSB, or GRU."

"We civilized and cultured people call it mercy—no doubt an alien concept to someone like you."

"As you'll soon find out, it was mistaken mercy on your part."

"Then bring it on. I can take whatever you can dish out."

"Not this time, comrade. Having obliterated your home, eviscerated your wealth, and reclaimed my wife, the rest will be easy … But not for you. After softening you up for a few days, we'll start with the vocal chords, which can be removed or simply burned away with acid. You're a singer, right? Well, you'll miss making and hearing music. After destroying your voice, one of my boys here will perforate your eardrums with an ice pick and obliterate your cochleae."

Unaccustomed to being outdone, but more to keep from meeting Cherkov's eyes and perhaps betraying his anxiety, Hap instead looked everywhere else to survey the room. It was filled with all manner of modern and medieval accoutrements of torture. Clearly, the equipment was an ominous sign of what was to come, but Hap tried as best he could to show no alarm. Worried there was little room for any last-minute brinkmanship, he could only guess how far Cherkov was willing to let this play out, especially when the beast in him was hungry and had to be fed. Well aware it would be hard to hide his visceral fear of such a man, Hap knew the extent of his suffering and perhaps survival demanded that he remain cagey but not too gutsy. Testing or running afoul of Cherkov's temper would only hasten the pace of what assuredly would be an agonizing endgame.

"Yes, do look around and take it all in, Franklin. As you can see, I can guarantee you a world of hurt long before the permanent maiming begins."

"This is quite an impressive collection of antiques you have here, Cherkov, and no doubt personally assembled by you."

"Right you are, as always. In fact, I rescued many of these old-fashioned ways of extracting information and confessions from Lubyanka when the KGB began administering drugs to replace the tried-and-true methods of torture."

"Before the fun begins, how about a last request?"

"Perhaps, Hap. I *can* call you Hap, right? What do you have in mind?"

"How about a final dry martini to ease the discomfort of what's ahead, but not that Russian Stoli swill you're drinking. I'd much prefer Boyd & Blair, a limited potato vodka made in Pittsburgh, but knowing that may not be available here, Grey Goose or even Absolut will do."

"That's a brilliant way to get started, Hap, but maybe it's time you were properly introduced to our beloved Stolichnaya."

Cherkov motioned to the guards. One grabbed Hap's head from behind and yanked it back while pinching his nose shut. The other forced open his jaw as Cherkov slowly approached—a full bottle and metal funnel in hand. After forcing the funnel deep into Hap's throat, he began pouring until there was no more.

"Welcome to waterboarding Russian style. Next time, we'll bring the vodka to a boil beforehand. Think of it as the beginning of the end. This can be an extended interrogation, which you know I'd prefer and enjoy, or an abbreviated one. It's all up to you. Misery can be optional if you'll answer one question."

"Then you'd better ask soon before the drunken stupor sets in."

"That's better, Hap. Seems you've already guessed what can be next for an uncooperative prisoner. I want to know what if anything the Americans know about Paradiso."

Given the circumstances and possible consequences, Hap knew that flippancy was probably not the best way to respond. It was hardly the time to be reckless no matter how strong the urge. Nevertheless, and true to character, the bias of his strong will and smart-ass personality overcame the danger of being captive prey.

"Paradiso? Isn't that the place where all good, God-fearing people are headed after death? It's life's final destination, where one can abide in everlasting harmony with one's Creator forever … like you will too, but in hell."

Unsurprised by Hap's defiance, Cherkov said nothing as his blank stare turned to a wicked smile. He stood and addressed the guards in their native tongue. Fortunately, Hap knew enough Russian to translate a portion of the instructions, and though fearing the beating he was about to take, he was gratified to learn that he would not be mutilated just yet. Intimidation was something he understood and could withstand, but maybe not what followed.

"Franklin, just so you know how serious this can get, how about a near-death experience to reinforce my sincerity and quicken your obedience? We call it the resurrection."

"Acquiescence has never come easily to me, so you'd best do what you must."

After a nod from Cherkov, one of the guards covered Hap's head with a plastic bag and cinched it tight around the neck while the other applied enough duct tape to ensure a secure, airtight seal. Gasping for breath, Hap saw Cherkov's smug smile through the clear plastic, but it soon turned foggy due to his gasping for air.

However gruesome it was to endure, asphyxiation didn't take long. Hap's panting stopped. The process could be reversed and life restored, but only if oxygen was available just prior to death's arrival. Possible complications might be a heart attack, seizure, or coma, but one other effect was long lasting and resulted in permanent impairment including memory loss. Unlike other less-sensitive parts of the body, brain tissue quickly starved and died when deprived of oxygenated blood.

Hap knew all this, and just prior to the delirium, he prayed to God that this would not be so. Once he passed out, the bag was quickly removed and CPR administered until he could again breathe. While heaving and coughing his way back to life, Hap was informed of something he already knew. Cherkov reminded him that an unfortunate side effect of his playing resurrection was that some brain loss had assuredly occurred and that repeating the procedure would result in much more each time. When finally able to speak, and as was his nature, Hap could not refrain from continuing his sarcastic humiliation in spite of the likely consequences.

"Saving my life shows a lot of compassion, Cherkov."

"We'll see if you can so easily shake off and survive what comes in the morning."

"I'll be right here waiting."

"What you might not know, Franklin, is that I've never failed to get a confession, and I don't expect to end that winning streak beginning with you."

"You may be surprised at my resilience."

"You have yet to experience the savagery I'm capable of, but you soon will."

Turning to his goons as he walked out, Cherkov issued fresh orders. "Suspend him. Use the boxing gloves. Give him a little taste of hell on earth. I want to see swelling and bruising but no blood when I return in the morning."

Given Cherkov's penchant for torture, Hap was surprised that Cherkov had departed and had left it to others to inflict the pain. Chains were lowered from pulleys attached to an overhead beam and attached to Hap's manacled hands. Once his feet were loosened from the chair, he was hoisted a few inches off the ground, and he became a defenseless punching bag for the blows that pummeled him from all sides. Just when he was certain his body could absorb no more, they lowered him to a seated position on the cold floor, where he collapsed into a pool of his own vomit that tasted of bitter bile cheapened by soured vodka.

Fearing he was finally in that place somewhere between life and death, but before losing consciousness, his mind raced through the obvious—*Where the fuck are my liberators?* He'd been chipped for just this kind of danger, and even if the damn thing couldn't emit a signal from what he presumed was a subterranean stronghold, precise tracking and mapping of his whereabouts had to have been known right up until he was taken belowground. Hap had never before been subjected to the kind of barbarism that he knew awaited him, and for the first time, he was fearful of losing his customary, brazen self-confidence. Desperation was no stranger; Hap had experienced and conquered it before, and he knew he must do so again. His period of reflective discernment ended; he worried more about how long his resolve would last if the cavalry didn't show up on time.

INTERROGATION GONE AWRY

HAP WASN'T SURE HOW MUCH TIME HAD PASSED when he was awakened by being doused with a bucket of numbing, cold water. At first, he could remember only that he had been dreaming, not what the dreams had been about—only fragments. He was certain they were not nightmares and clearly not the one he was about to face while conscious. The shivering returned as he slowly realized where he was and who had arrived to dish out more punishment.

"Good morning, Hap. You look good in black and blue."

"I'm happy you find them such flattering colors. It's a real tribute to your boys, who did their best to bring out the worst in me."

"To reward them for such good work, I'm thinking of letting them have their way with Louise."

"You wouldn't."

"Why should I not make sure that her last memory before surgery is an unpleasant one that she can reflect on for months during her painful recuperation?"

Another two black-clad commandos entered. They were alike in every way to the pair who had beaten him and had stood guard since Hap's arrival.

"Meet the day shift, Franklin. These are fresh recruits to spell the ones who softened you up yesterday and kept watch until my return. It's now time for the night shift to sleep, but perhaps not dismissing them before enjoying a free-rein tasting of Louise. In fact, maybe you and I could watch."

"Look, Cherkov, I've come here alone and willingly, done what you've asked, and answered your question. If you want to further torture me for your own sick reasons, suit yourself, but I have nothing else for you."

"That part could be over if you'd cooperate, so let's start afresh, shall we?"

"Why not? It's the way I approach every day."

"To avoid a lot more of what you experienced yesterday, why don't you just tell me everything the Yanks know about Paradiso?"

"We've been through that. I don't know a damn thing. Beyond blaming me for taking Louise from you, I'm having trouble connecting all the other dots regarding this little caper of yours. You probably know I'm retired and no longer a player on the dark stage, so why not interrogate someone else who is?"

"One last time, Franklin … Paradiso."

"And for the last time, how can I tell you anything about something I have no knowledge of?"

"Maybe pulling out all your fingernails will refresh your memory, but don't worry. You'll recover from any minor mutilation in time to witness Louise's long convalescence. Now before that, and as an act of good faith, let's loosen your bonds and allow you some free movement while you think some more about amending your response."

The new guards attached what looked like a choke chain around his neck but was really an improvised shock collar. Once the other shackles were removed, Hap struggled to his feet, and though knowing what would come next, he nevertheless lunged at one of the guards in hopes of securing his pistol. The initial shock felled him in midstride. Though the convulsions lasted no more than a few seconds, the result was complete incapacitation. When again able to move, and in defiance, Hap somehow managed to stand and approach his captor, but when he got too close, Cherkov again pushed the remote control delivering a second shock. That time, it lasted longer, and the voltage had been cranked up. Unable to control his bladder amid the debilitation, he had no resistance to what followed.

"Franklin, I see you've pissed all over the floor. Maybe next time you'll shit yourself, and just think—all for my amusement."

"You're one lurid, sick fuck."

"Easy now or I'll use the clicker on you again until you're a well-trained dog. Now that you've had your little taste of freedom, it's time to step it up a bit."

Cherkov walked to a long table laden with all manner of torturous devices and chose what looked like a cattle prod. He nodded to one of the guards, who attached its trailing wire to a series of car batteries. Hap had already seen such a contraption and knew what was ahead. Called a *picana*, it could deliver a punishingly high-voltage but low-current shock to various parts of the body, especially the most sensitive areas. The outcome was far more effective when the recipient was drenched with water as a conductor to lower the electrical resistance. It was a primitive but effective way to extract confessions. Hap knew that they were still in use by Mexican drug kingpins to root out informants and that the procedure never failed to produce the desired result. A proven barbaric degenerate, Cherkov would be aware that dousing the subject with water intensified the pain and prolonged its agony.

"This could be a lot easier if you'd stop resisting me, Franklin. In your case, it's the smart move. You should know that capitulation to a more powerful combatant is not always a sign of weakness. In fact, peaceful subjugation has been going on since the beginning of time, when men began ruling other men."

"That'll soon be passé in a world governed by democracy."

"Not if *my* president has his way and turns the clock back to a time when people welcomed despotic rulers rather than starve."

Once Hap was doused with another bucket of water to reduce the skin's resistance to accepting the current, Cherkov approached with the picana in hand. Hap's last thought was that neither

Thomas Edison nor George Westinghouse could have imagined that their early research into electricity would eventually produce such an instrument. Things had gone awry, there was no conceivable escape, and Hap had nobody to blame but himself.

Upon regaining consciousness, Hap found himself again strapped to the chair. In front of him was a table bearing four items—three round objects and what looked like a red ski sock on which the hammer and sickle emblem of the former Soviet Union was embroidered. It wasn't long before his curiosity was satisfied.

"Since it's only fair to share what's ahead of you, Hap, let me introduce you to another of my relics from the dungeons of Lubyanka. What we in the KGB often called the Fabergé eggs is nothing more than a trio of iron cannonballs weighing one, two, and three pounds along with some smaller steel ball bearings. When put into a sock, they can deliver quite a wallop and more damage than a brass-knuckled blow from my helpers here. I'm sure you understand the physics of centrifugal force, which escalates almost exponentially when the acceleration and weight are increased. The radius of rotation is a factor too in elevating the pain level, which is why we'll be using this nice long knee sock. You might think of it as a novel way of getting stoned but without the high."

Knowing that a defiant inmate usually fared better and lived longer in captivity than an acquiescent one, Hap was prepared to keep on gambling. And of all people, he was not about to let Cherkov get the best of him, at least not just yet. With his customary aplomb and reservoir of resistance nearly depleted, he nevertheless summoned enough remaining strength to mock his captor one last time.

"One request, Cherkov—I hope there will be appropriate music to accompany this deep tissue massage of yours. Stravinsky would be nice especially since he rejected your common homeland

and became an American citizen. Given today's occasion, how about *Petrushka* or *The Rite of Spring*?"

"Unfortunately not, but you'll soon be singing your own song of woe. We won't be striking your head, which will allow your brain to fully process and feel the misery more acutely. What my men stuff into the sock will be carefully selected based on both their ballistic properties and the targeted area in order to break all bones and joints near the surface such as fingers, toes, elbows, knees, shoulders, ribs, and spine. If you are able to listen closely instead of crying out, you'll be able to hear the crunching of your own skeleton. Eventually, paralysis will set in and any pain will disappear. Within an hour or two, your skin will turn black and blue from your neck to your feet. If by chance you survive, you'll spend the rest of your life in a wheelchair or therapy learning how to use your new prosthetic limbs."

BREAKOUT

GIVING UP IN DESPERATION WASN'T A CHOICE. Louise thought about what Hap would do if in jeopardy with no way out—he would think until a solution came to him. So that's what she did. After thinking until she was sure her brain was sweating, one novel possibility eventually percolated, and at first seemed so obvious.

For once in her life, Weezie was happy to be a big-busted gal whose ample bosom required a sturdy underwire bra to keep things in their proper place. A woman of modesty, Weezie's intention was never to amplify, enhance, or showcase the view for others, but at her age, simply to keep them from heading too far south. This time, the underwire would serve a far different purpose that might save her life. Weezie's rigorous Pilates regimen had enabled her to stretch in ways most others could only dream of. So despite the handcuffs, she was able to wriggle out of her bra and bring it to her mouth. After finding the end of the underwire, she nibbled at the fabric until the seam was opened, and then she pulled the wire out with her teeth.

What an odd coincidence that it had been Hap who had shown her how to pick a lock and made her do that several times until she had a burglar's knack for it. At first, the wire wasn't thick or strong enough to pick the handcuffs, but after doubling and braiding it by twisting the strands together, it proved to be as good as her jailor's key. Within a minute, both cuffs were off, making it easy to work her magic on the set that bound her ankles. Once free, she attacked the cell's lock, which proved more difficult. It required something more rigid to release, so she again twisted more of the wire together for strength.

Hearing Hap's screams provided her more than enough motivation to realize that his life was dependent on her escape. Her trembling hands made it difficult, but the lock finally gave way and the cell door swung open. On the guard's table was a submachine gun carelessly left by one of her captors. Though unfamiliar with how it operated, she carried it like a soldier might when under fire. Following the howling sounds, she approached the source until discovering the torture chamber and coming face to face with the horror within. Peering in, she shuddered at the macabre sight of Hap strapped to the elevated chair. Though awake and alive, he looked like roadkill. Apparently taking a break from their interrogation, the Russians were seated and talking quietly. Being caught off guard was something they hadn't expected.

"Stand up, turn around, and face the wall!" she commanded.

At first, Cherkov and his men just stared at each other in mocking disbelief, but Weezie immediately recognized that knowing look—the kind men signaled when they didn't believe their opponent capable of taking the next step. Weezie was no fool, and in a display of what would surely follow if they didn't obey, she sprayed the wall above their heads with a fusillade of rounds before releasing the trigger. The outburst got their attention once her surprisingly brazen message was delivered.

"Guess you boys now understand that I'm one mother you'd better not fuck with. Hands up high," she barked in a newly found voice that even Louise failed to recognize as her own. Unsure if her demeanor came naturally or from watching too many Westerns as a kid, she nevertheless found it exhilarating and continued in her cowboy gunslinger role play.

One by one she demanded each to disarm himself and kick any weapon over to her. Once collected, but keeping her gun trained on them at all times, she released Hap from his bonds.

Though somewhat disoriented, he stood, stretched, and hobbled to gather his clothing.

Cherkov didn't know it, but he was damn lucky to be facing the wall instead of Louise. If not, he would have been unable to keep from smirking, which would have infuriated her. With a warm gun in her hands that was loaded and lethal, it was now she who was in charge. Ex-husband or not, given what Dmitri had planned for her face, it was all she could do to refrain from finally ridding herself of him for good. She even hoped he might offer the least provocation if only to test her capacity to take a life.

Louise knew from her research that killing was one of those primal urges that most people experienced, but it certainly wasn't one she had ever felt before. Having memorized the Ten Commandments in Sunday school, she knew the endings of all that began with "Thou shalt not …" More important, she had been taught that such prohibitions were for enduring moral resonance, especially in times such as this. She also worried that taking a life might jeopardize her salvation. Conflicted as she was, Louise nevertheless decided the commandments were intended as mandates to abide and live by. It was obvious that Hap had not arrived at the same conclusion as evident when interrupting her thoughts with his instructions.

"Weeze, much to my relief, I see you have a sound recall of your father's early firearms training, but this is for keeps, so if any one of them so much as flinches, mow 'em all down."

Once dressed, Hap proceeded to hog-tie each of them in a way that would stretch the sinews of their arms and legs until they were as taut as piano wire. With Weezie left standing guard, he followed the warren of passages back to their beginning. Finding the staircase, he climbed only high enough until his cell phone reception was restored so he could call in the team for rescue. Even before the call went through, the chip between his toes broadcast his precise coordinates to Langley.

Hap figured help would arrive within the hour, so he was surprised when a black-clad team burst into the bunker within minutes. More men in black was never a good sign, and when not recognizing any of them as his people, Hap instinctively covered Weezie with his body as the shooting began. Cherkov was spared, but his guards were summarily taken down. From their mannerisms and speech, Hap easily identified the new arrivals as Russian even before the leader began in near-flawless but stilted English with a Slavic tinge.

"Mr. Franklin, please let me explain or at least convey what I'm authorized to say. We want only the doctor. She'll be under house arrest until all this is settled, but that housing will be an elegantly appointed dacha outside Moscow where she will be treated as a dignified guest of our president. As to Comrade Cherkov and you, we've been instructed to let the two of you settle this between yourselves once and for all. May the best man win. We assume that will be you, Mr. Franklin, and in very short order. We will not interfere and have no interest in the outcome. As far as the Kremlin is concerned, both of you are expendable."

"When will she be returned to the United States?"

"Once an equitable diplomatic solution is reached. Until then, she will be safe from harm, but knowing your team is on the way, we must now go."

It was all too clear that these were FSB agents on direct assignment by the czar. On the surface, it made little immediate sense to Hap. He wondered why they hadn't just taken or eliminated all three of their own and left Louise with him. After gathering her luggage and injecting Louise with a mild sedative, they gently helped her to her feet and withdrew, leaving Hap and Cherkov alone with little time to spare.

RETRIBUTION

Awaiting his own team's arrival and beset with rage, Hap could easily have finished off Cherkov while he remained hog-tied, but that wouldn't provide him the satisfaction he sought. Instead, and despite his weakened state, he stupidly chose to make it a fair fight by releasing Cherkov from his bondage. As he did so, Cherkov was the first to speak.

"You're crazy to do this, Franklin, and you will soon be sorry you did."

"Russian roulette would be a faster solution for ridding this world of you once and for all, but as you well know, I'm a believer in fair play, which makes me the better man."

"Sanctimonious to the end. Well then, I'll be sure Louise will learn of that difference between us … And how it ended for you."

Hap worried that he had made a foolhardy blunder, but also knew that because the body was governed by the brain, it was capable of astonishing feats if motivated. Summoning all his remaining strength and helped along with a surge of adrenalin, he hoped to prevail in what would be a last-ditch struggle for survival. Years earlier, Hap could kill with numbing efficiency, but he wasn't so sure anymore.

Despite daily calisthenics, he was no longer in prime shape, and on days like this, his body would let him know that. But his agility was never better, and when Cherkov lunged, Hap caught him with a vicious uppercut to the jaw, and while reeling from the initial blow, Hap began a relentless beating until the Russian dropped.

Bolstered by a newfound surge of resentment, he decided to take it one step further. Since Weezie had nearly been raped and had been about to be surgically disfigured, Hap felt entitled to a little butchering of his own. He thrust the picana into Cherkov's groin to immobilize him. Once the Russian's wailings had subsided, Hap grabbed the double-bladed meat ax from the table. "Comrade, you will never again raise a hand to me or anyone else."

Hap brought the ax down with all his might to make a clean cut above Cherkov's right wrist. With Cherkov writhing in pain and watching, Hap then took a hammer to the dismembered hand and pulverized the severed fingers and palm ensuring that they could never be surgically reattached. Overwhelmed with fatigue, Hap slumped into the wingchair that his captor had once used.

Reflecting on the sobering sight and taking in the full measure of his own brutality, Hap wondered if Weezie had been right when she once compared him to Cherkov due to their many shared traits. If she were, then maybe Hap had crossed the line and was becoming no more than a shadowy reflection of his nemesis. He hoped not, but he knew otherwise, and he was certain he'd be praying for his soul's redemption for a long time. Having succumbed to his innermost base desires, Hap considered his dismemberment of Cherkov as not much different from the torture the Russian had inflicted. The only distinction was in the degree to which Hap could resist the temptation to take it too far beyond the bounds of a fair fight. But this was not the time to be conflicted, particularly when there was no proven antidote for remorse. He decided that such reflections could wait until the broader mission was over and Weezie was safe.

Bud's band of recruited mercenaries arrived. The leader and first one through the door could not help but gasp at the shocking scene. The carnage alone was disturbing, but it couldn't compare with the vast inventory of torturous implements on display. None of that stopped them from getting right to work. Their job was a quick extraction without assessing what had gone down.

"Mr. Franklin, what hath God wrought here?" the leader asked.

"God had nothing to do with this. What you see is justice having been served."

"Looks more like vengeance."

"But tinged with a dose of mercy. After all, I could more easily have just killed him, but we're charged with bringing the bastard back alive."

"Damn, Hap, we were looking forward to a nice little skirmish here, but it seems you cheated us out of that. Did you mop this all up by yourself?"

"No, I had help, but that's all the intel you'll be getting from me."

The field medic tied off Cherkov's stump to prevent his bleeding out and further shock. Another helped by shooting up the fresh amputee with morphine to dull the insufferable pain and squelch his moaning. Field combat being what it was, both had seen such injuries before in Afghanistan and were battle worn if not insensitive to those involving loss of limb or even the occasional decapitation. Their job was to make sure Cherkov could tolerate being loaded quietly into the disguised delivery van out front for transport to the hospital at the Chièvres Air Base.

After retrieving what remained of Weezie's belongings and scouring the dungeon for anything else that might provide a clue as to what had happened there, the men in black escorted Hap and Cherkov to the van and sped away. Apart from the blood and gore, what remained were Cherkov's two dead soldiers of fortune.

Once Hap's team had safely reached the military compound, the cleanup crews would be called in. Discarding the bodies was the easiest part. After zipped up in bags, Cherkov's henchmen would be delivered to a crematorium that had an unspoken arrangement with the CIA. Oddly enough, since both sides had such agreements in place around the world, any given furnace might be on retainer by both the Russian and American intelligence services. Following removal, a second crew—the scrubbers and cleaners—would be summoned to sanitize the entire place of any trace of who had been there and what had gone down.

When Bud learned of the mission's outcome, he was furious at Hap for going it alone and only somewhat pleased with the outcome. But before dealing with the aftermath, he first had to authorize payment to the Brussels subcontractors who had taken out the trash and performed the cleansing. Though neither side could afford having the details of what had occurred in the bunker known by any others, Bud wasn't about to foot the bill for Russians killing Russians. Unusual as it might be, he simply told the contractors to put the charges on the FSB's tab. Though often strained, Bud had an almost friendly rapport with his counterpart at Lubyanka Square from having worked together when situations like this one demanded an unlikely collaboration. At certain levels, as when their presidents spoke on the hotline between the White House and Kremlin, relationships between Russians and Americans were not always adversarial. It proved not to be in this case either. Since most of the mess and both riddled bodies were the handiwork of the FSB, once the request was made, the Russian spymaster was happy to accept the charges.

ALL ABOARD

AFTER A BRIEF RECUPERATION AT CHIÈVRES, Cherkov was relocated to Ramstein Air Base, which was by far the largest of the 174 permanent US military installations in Germany. The sprawling 3,000-acre base was home to more than 55,000 US servicemen and a few permanent interrogators on the agency's payroll. Now referred to only by his code name—Rasputin—Cherkov was kept there in isolation for a complete convalescence together with unending rounds of questioning that began only after the pain and trauma from losing his appendage had subsided. His experienced inquisitors knew they could exact better answers only after he was well enough to feel the fresh discomfort from their activities.

Because Rasputin was once right-handed, he required some therapy to make the adjustment to performing all tasks with his left, which included brushing his teeth, picking his nose, and wiping his ass. Such simple procedures became especially difficult after the middle finger of his left hand was accidentally broken after he used it as a response when first questioned. That severely limited other activities including attempts at self-gratification, which at that time was no doubt the least of his worries but might become a welcome relief later.

The short-term goal of Cherkov's incarceration was to coerce him into disclosing everything about Paradiso; confessions about his other egregious misdeeds could be extracted when time was not of the essence. After unspeakably harsh methods of persuasion, and once the sadistic but accomplished jailors were satisfied he had coughed up everything, the prisoner known only as

Rasputin was transferred again. That time, it would be to a place of possible permanence whose secret location was known only by a few, was on no map, and had no known fixed coordinates.

Its registry bore a Panamanian flag, but the vessel was effectively owned by the CIA and unofficially dubbed the Ghost Ship. Originally christened as a seaworthy but small container ship, it had been repurposed at considerable taxpayer expense as a floating prison. With no assigned destination, it would appear on radar to be drifting aimlessly though always just beyond US territorial boundaries. America had learned its lesson from Guantanamo, so to preserve its legal rights and keep what went on aboard ship from any who might be curious, it remained at sea, where it was refueled as necessary. Though hardly impregnable, its invincibility came from being hidden in plain sight. Few had access to witness what happened aboard, but everyone at Langley knew it was no cruise line and hardly a place where the milk of human kindness flowed freely if at all.

This was not Cherkov's first voyage as a first-class passenger. He had been imprisoned there once before and knew the drill all too well. Despite that knowledge, he was living proof that like arrogance, recidivism was hard to shake. As before, his stateroom was a thick-walled steel shipping cargo container welded to the deck that, while familiar to him, hardly felt like home. Painted black, it absorbed heat from the sun's radiance by day and drew the chill of its absence by night. Ventilation was limited to a small opening in the wall secured by a latticed grating of steel bars. His bare feet remained manacled and chained to allow limited movement just shy of being able to reach the walls. Beyond a straw pallet, the only other amenities were a basin of salt water to wash and a slop pot for everything else. Both were emptied only every three days to keep the flies away if only temporarily. Only when he was cooperative would the sea water be exchanged for fresh water and the other pot replaced with a clean one.

Inasmuch as possible, treatment of enemy combatants was aboveboard, but not above reproach. The days of sweating out information under a hot lamp were long gone and replaced by far more effective if often overly coercive and brutal means. Soon, an unspoken understanding developed between prisoner and captor that had all to do with choosing comfort or discomfort. Anything else, like attempting escape or praying for rescue, was just false hope.

It began with sleep and light deprivation, which fooled the body into believing it should be asleep when it wasn't. Combined with the excruciating heat and weight loss from limited rations, the enhanced interrogation techniques worked as they always had, and the formerly recalcitrant prisoner grew more compliant as time passed. At first, he was unwilling to provide any confirmation of the claims made by the hardened agents who questioned him, but once more draconian measures were undertaken, Rasputin's resistance and recalcitrance eventually waned.

Of utter importance was the extraction of information that could destroy Paradiso. By that time, its location had been discovered, and one of Bud's teams had learned from the head troll that only Cherkov controlled the kill switch, which could be activated or in this case deactivated only by a multidigit code or retinal eye scan. When threatened with removal of his eyeball without anesthesia and the promise of leaving the empty eye socket vulnerable to infection, Cherkov finally coughed up the code.

Little by little, he revealed all the particulars of his nefarious activities, and some of them came as a surprise and complete shock to those back at Langley who vetted the taped confessions. Eventually, they would get from him what they wanted, and his life would be spared for another day's reckoning. Rasputin knew they would stop short of killing him, but he hoped he would not be returned to the czar to face the same fate his namesake had.

Once certain that nobody beyond Cherkov knew the code for the ultimate kill switch, several of Bud's people assisted by a boatload of Marines and Special Forces began dismantling the Paradiso complex. Disarming the explosives came first, followed by crating all the electronic gadgetry and ferrying it to an armed navy ship that had been disguised when constructed as a large fishing trawler.

What they found first was enough ordnance to blow the small island off the map. The island itself didn't really matter, but the contents of the elaborate maze of buildings would be precious cargo indeed for the likes of the CIA's silent partners in Silicon Valley. Such material would normally be passed off to the NSA, which was supposedly the country's digital locksmith entrusted with safeguarding the internet, but not this time. The haul from Paradiso would remain the province of the CIA, an equally skilled electronic lock picker especially when it came to compromising other nations' secrets.

Because all of it still posed a risk of accidental detonation, removal was slow and deliberate. During the process, Paradiso's resident trolls were taken prisoner for their own safety and ultimate value. Though warm-blooded catch, they were stowed where fish normally would be—berthed belowdecks in the hold until transferred elsewhere for processing. Though not necessarily guileless, they were nevertheless complicit in the Russians' attempted digital coup, and after months of interrogation aboard an incredibly special ship in international waters, some or all might be charged and sentenced for war crimes. Of course, another and far wiser path would be to co-opt them into reassembling a version of Paradiso somewhere else for America's own cybergames. There was no reason that now uncovered, Paradise Found should become Paradise Lost.

TRADING PLACES

GETTING SPIES BACK WHOSE DIPLOMATIC IMMUNITY had been revoked was one thing, but exchanging obscure political prisoners on trumped-up charges was quite another. Trading Weezie for a wretch like Dmitri Cherkov made good sense, but the folks who made such decisions weren't sure this one was a fair deal. At face value, it wasn't. The proposed plan of getting a research doc back in exchange for the release of an international weapons dealer, global cybercriminal, and killer would play to an unsympathetic audience. Hap suspected it might be a hard sell, so he needed to put himself into the mix. Though just a doc, Weezie was clearly not a plain vanilla one, and somebody at the very top needed to know that. There would be a steep price of admission for enlisting the incumbent president's help and especially so close to the election, but in this situation, Hap would have sold his soul to gain the president's agreement.

Getting an audience with one of the president's men came with no outright upfront cost, but every interaction with the White House thereafter involved monetizing the expected quid pro quo. The commerce of trading favors had become commonplace, and it was no secret that this administration had taken pay to play far beyond the playground. Hap soon got a nauseating dose of it close up. Instead of discussing the diplomatic merits of granting Hap's humanitarian request, the sole focus was on how much ransom he could afford to pay for Weezie's life. Once they had vetted Hap further and determined what the real amount should be, it was doubled from the first estimate. It was no different from any other of the nonnegotiable deals the president had once called artful.

Due to the urgency of Hap's petition, the ransom was converted to yet an even higher amount. Another disturbing term was that the full amount had to be made upfront in untraceable currency before the president would consider any involvement. The message was overt; there was no room for bargaining, and it was no more than bribery.

Though indignant, Hap was a big boy who knew how the world worked, and he would comply, but he privately vowed to get even one day. The president's bag man must have sensed this and would see to it that Weezie's return would be delayed by extended negotiations with the Russians. The intention was that it be just long enough to send Hap a message not to fuck with the president, especially one who was close to being shown the door.

The agreed-upon dead drop was the open-air Jefferson Memorial in Washington. Hap was to put the oversized suitcase on the marble floor at the base of Thomas Jefferson's statue and walk away. When packing the thousands of Benjamins, which was what drug dealers were now calling hundred-dollar bills, Hap could not help but think that he was sullying the Franklin name by agreeing to the extortion.

For the State Department, shadowboxing with the Russians over Weezie was fast becoming a diplomatic nightmare. Starved for political capital, the czar needed plenty of cover on this one or his iron grip on the motherland might be pried loose by the growing movement afoot to oppose him. His public forbearance notwithstanding, he was no doubt seething in private and wanted an end to this at all costs. Expectedly, it was the American president who eventually gave him an easy way out.

Since neither side wanted to blink first, negotiations became more protracted and tortuous than they otherwise could have been. Repatriation was always complicated, and this time, the last thorny obstacle was pride. As in any pissing contest, both parties remained truculent, with each needing to emerge from the impasse claiming a win, though there was no public audience to applaud the victor.

Even with the confiscation of Paradiso's intricate computer network—a fact the CIA would never admit—unwinding the transactional labyrinth of financial swindles might take forever, and certainly longer than the US was willing to be patient. Instead, it demanded an immediate payment of $1.5 billion in restitution and an additional half-billion in compensatory damages. The amount would cover the claims of only what had been bilked from Americans; the czar would be responsible for settling any claims by foreigners directly.

Two billion was a small price for keeping the entire fiasco quiet, and following a confidential conversation with his American counterpart, the czar himself interceded and agreed to terms acceptable to both sides. Of course, few if any would ever know what was secretly ceded to the czar in return; trading favors in the dark had become emblematic of the cozy relationship between the two leaders.

Over the CIA's objection, it was decided to take the Russian president's word that determining Cherkov's fate would be swift and better executed on Russian soil than saddling the American courts and penal system with needless expense. Sparing a public trial would mean the administration would not have to admit to the existence of an active cyberwarfare with a sworn enemy or, and more important, that a war had nearly been lost.

Once all financial assets plundered from Hap and others by Cherkov were restored, the prisoner exchange would take place. Following his three-month-long confinement aboard the Ghost Ship, Cherkov would be returned to the czar in chains. That would be the second time he would be sent home in shame, and the czar wasn't known for granting second chances. To do so would be embarrassing and foolish, neither of which he welcomed if news of such a pardon was ever leaked at home. More humiliating would be if it played out on a world stage, where he would lose face among the same leaders he needed to continue impressing with his ruthlessness.

Unbeknown to Hap, the seventh floor thought it was a mistake but was powerless to oppose it. The only good outcome was that Weezie's safe return in exchange for Cherkov was assured by the czar himself, and that was more than enough.

SPECIAL DELIVERY

T HE EXCHANGE WAS MADE without much warning or fanfare. Weezie was flown to Andrews AFB aboard one of Aeroflot's special planes that were kept in reserve for such use and bore no logo, identification, or adornment beyond a tail number. Arriving under cover of darkness, the secret flight didn't taxi to a gate or hanger; it was met on a remote tarmac by three black SUVs whose passengers included Hap, Bud, and a heavily armed security detail. By agreement, they waited in their vehicles until Weezie was escorted down the stairs along with her luggage. Part of the bargain was that she be personally examined by Hap before Cherkov was released from armed captivity in another SUV parked some distance away. Once cued by her captors, Hap ran to her as others trailed behind to gather her belongings. Weezie hugged him and wouldn't release her embrace for a long time.

All the while, Hap was careful to shield her sight from the prisoner she was being traded for. His identity concealed by a hooded jumpsuit, the one-handed figure was force-marched to the foot of the staircase before the ankle shackles were removed and he was permitted to board the plane. Cherkov knew his fate was all but certain, but before the door closed, he turned around for one final look at Hap, and in defiance of the agreed-upon departure protocol, he beckoned Hap closer. Upon reaching the bottom of the stairway and despite the noise of the idling jet engines, Hap was close enough to hear Rasputin's parting taunt. As always, it was delivered with a contemptuous and sanctimonious sneer.

"Franklin, you know I'm invincible, right?"

"You'd better hope not, comrade, because if you survive what's ahead, you won't find me as merciful the next time."

When Hap joined the rest of the American detail on the tarmac, Bud demanded to know what had been said between them in private. His response was that Cherkov had only wished him well and that Hap had bidden him goodbye and told him that he hoped the long flight would be pleasant. Bud's disappointed look of incredulity was further punctuated with his typical response of "Bullshit!"

Hap insisted that Weezie's preliminary debriefing could wait. That night, she would be taken to her own home and allowed to rest in comfortable, familiar surroundings before being requested to relive the trauma of the last few months. She remained all but mute during the hour-long trip to Baltimore, never letting go of Hap's hand or lifting her head from his shoulder. It was a sign of inexpressible exhaustion, a condition Hap had become very familiar with when returning from distant covert assignments.

When they arrived, Louise was clearly unsteady on her feet, so Hap carried her to the master suite and gingerly placed her in bed. As he turned the lights off, she uttered her first words, which were weak and full of apprehension. "Hap, you won't leave, will you?"

"Of course not. You just rest. I'll brew you some sleepy time tea to help make that happen."

Maintaining his vigil through the night, Hap sprawled out on a nearby couch, but he was kept awake by the unaccustomed pattern of her fitful sleep. At Hap's suggestion, Bud had arranged for her kitchen to be stocked with groceries to last for a week. Fresh-cut flowers in every room provided a mix of intoxicating fragrances and highlighted Mother Nature's way of affirming life. He also had made Bud promise that a large bouquet of lavender would be in her bedroom ... but without giving a reason.

PART VI:
Finale

RECOVERY

A S EXPECTED, WEEZIE'S ROAD TO RECOVERY was longer than Hap's. Her rehabilitation included regular home visits by one of Langley's best psychiatrists, who found working on the mind of another shrink somewhat of a challenge. Hap was advised to keep his distance except by phone until she was done processing what had happened and could dispel the demons.

As they had with defense contractors and the savviest of tech companies, those at the top levels of the federal government had long-standing, cozy relationships with the heads of many leading universities and particularly those with key research capabilities. A medical juggernaut, Johns Hopkins had been on that list for a long time and was rewarded through generous grants from agencies like the NIH and CDC. Such relationships were maintained only at the most senior levels and never required or included any written agreements or traceable communication.

First, a cover story to fit the expected time of Weezie's absence was crafted; the spin on it was unmistakably the work of some bright analyst at Langley. Soon after the call was made, Johns Hopkins quietly announced that Dr. Porter had been granted an extended working sabbatical. What was not acknowledged was that her leave of absence was at full pay along with a hefty discretionary supplement for her research while not on campus. None of her colleagues would ever know that she had been in service to the country and its national security.

Before the shrinks gave her a clean bill of health, Louise found that simply working in her garden provided the best therapy. It had been overrun with weeds during her absence, but she soon rectified that while adding the plantings she had always longed to cultivate. A passionate gardener, she was equally at home in blue jeans, a peasant blouse, and a straw hat as she was when attired in a glamorous evening gown and bedecked with expensive and bedazzling jewelry.

Her honesty and commitment when on all fours in the dirt was something Hap had always found alluring. He wished he could see it with his own eyes, but he had to make do with hearing about the garden's progress during their daily call. It wasn't long before Hap could tell that the spring had returned to her step. The best gauge was the welcome return of her playful wit and risqué banter, which to him signaled a near full recovery.

Louise too was convinced she was ready to return. After Brussels and Moscow, she needed the comfort found in her life's former routine—the kind of conventional normalcy she could deal with. Given the newfound luxury of having time to do little but reflect on the past, she had spent most of it retracing her friendship with Hap back to its beginning. From its infancy during their very first slow dance in seventh grade, it all seemed right, though she knew that some parts were all wrong. Running it through her mind like a double feature on a continuous loop, she often hit the pause button to savor the best parts. Sometimes she wondered if he was doing the same thing.

Their lovemaking alone had been a virtual travelogue all by itself and one that Louise had often replayed in her mind. From their first encounter in Bar Harbor to the soft sand dunes of a secluded Cape Cod beach, the warm winter surf of Cabo San Lucas, the moss-cushioned ground of Fox Chapel's Trillium Trail, and when blanketed under the glow of crimson fall sunsets along the eastern shore, the locales were many and varied. In the finest hotels and those that were simply convenient, they had enjoyed extended stays and a host of abbreviated but adventuresome quickies.

Some of those reminiscences sparked outright laughter, like the night they had spent in an out-of-the-way bed and breakfast in the Maryland countryside. When unable to muffle the screeching sounds from the antique bedsprings, they moved in desperation to the floor, which ended up creaking too. Other of their amusing antics came to mind, but one stood out from all the others. On a daring bet, they managed to accomplish what they thought only teenagers could do but in a more imaginative way—in his car and hers alike. Afterward, Hap had admitted that after crossing that one off the bucket list, there was no reason on earth to attempt it again.

For Weezie, of course, it was Tuscany that was among her favorite memories, or at least until the very end. Their mutual intoxication with each other when in Italy was not much different than an alcoholic's hangover from booze, when perhaps the best tonic was a hair of the dog that bit them. At least that was the reasoning Hap offered Weezie before what became their requisite morning romp.

Following their separation for so many years, their now decade-long relationship had been more like a partnership of equal parity, one that provided each of them far more than the usual reciprocal benefits. Real intimacy came from sharing all of life's details—the hopes, struggles, and failures real and imagined. Sometimes, the satisfaction came from long walks, talks, or just cuddling through the night. Maybe what they had was all there ever would be, and anything beyond that was never meant to be. If so, Louise might learn to be satisfied with that, but she would always long for more.

HIDDEN IN PLAIN SIGHT

U NLIKE LOUISE, WHO HAD REMAINED in self-isolation under Langley's orders, Hap had no such restrictions, but he had been given strong recommendations that he more or less followed. Maintaining a low profile while staying at his home on the Chesapeake was a good start. The FBI was already keeping an eye on both a former vice president and defense secretary who lived nearby, so adding Hap to their babysitting list for a few weeks was easy for Bud to arrange. As Hap knew from years of undercover surveillance, sometimes hiding in plain sight provided the best cover. Exiled on the bay wasn't harsh duty, but Hap was anxious to get on with life and return to Pittsburgh, where he could more easily restore what had once been his life. Nevertheless, he busied himself by sailing or working the often-neglected grounds by day and reading at night.

Fearing the potential cognitive loss from Cherkov's little game of resurrection, and because he couldn't just talk it over with his doctor, one evening Hap did what he always did by serving up a slice of self-help from the internet. Though always skeptical of what he found there, he reluctantly began augmenting if not substituting what he normally ate with loads of brain food. Fortunately, most of it was tasty and part of his usual diet—coffee, dark chocolate, blueberries, olive oil, broccoli, and oranges. A few others not quite as palatable but nonetheless edible included oily fish, avocados, and beets. All Hap knew was that the brain represented only 3 percent of the body's weight but consumed twenty percent of its energy. It seemed only logical to him that fueling it with high octane would enhance his neurological circuitry.

Scientists might never know how many neurons would have to fire at once for that to occur, but Hap was more than willing to supercharge his diet to help the process along. Another remedy he had witnessed firsthand from his mother's late-stage dementia was the power of music. It would not arrest but could delay certain cognitive deficits by stimulating and triggering other parts of her memory that overlapped. It also gave him a welcome clinical reason to boost any benefit from the brain food by surrounding himself with music ... even if always played too loud.

Surfing the internet for things like recommended brain food was one thing, as all a snooper might discover would be someone's browsing history enabling an automatic reshuffling of tailored popup ads. However, using most any other device and particularly those that communicated with each other or shared that information invited unwelcome danger.

Despite his fascination with all the new electronic gizmos, Hap knew they were risky to use, especially given his line of side work. The technological era had ushered in an easy way to spy. A little-known fact was that everyone around the globe who used a smartphone was vulnerable to an array of pernicious network connections. This was one of the reasons criminals and often the CIA used old-timey burner phones that were stupid but harmless on their own. Flip phones also permitted the user to easily remove the battery from the back to assure the phone was completely off and not just sleeping. When disabled in that fashion, it could not listen, spy through imbedded apps, or reveal its location in relation to the nearest cell tower. Thankfully, this was something Hap could do without bellying up to the genius bar at an Apple store.

Some were better at mining information than others, but that list didn't yet include the US of A. Once harvested, compromised information was sold to the highest bidder or simply stolen by others for indiscriminate uses. It had long been in the mutual interests of both the government and major tech companies to conceal these vast data-collection efforts from the public, but safety wasn't one of those interests. Washington kept ignoring the repeated warnings of the intelligence services, but as was the case with most of the important things, it preferred to kick that can down the road and out of public sight.

The bevy of sophisticated toys from the Silicon Valley brain trusts was not unlike the Amazon Echo Hap had been given by his youngest sister for his last birthday. Though portable, it found a place of permanence on his desk in the study, and it was used mostly to play better-amplified music of his preference from his laptop. Inevitably, that resulted in songs from the forties, fifties, and sixties, which Hap believed were the only three decades when good music had been written during the last century.

Other Echo applications Hap routinely enjoyed included some that read aloud the headlines of the major newspapers, provided a spoken weather forecast, searched the internet for answers to his esoteric queries, and made phone calls on command. Sometimes, there were those forgetful occasions when Hap's confusion result-ed in wrongful identity as when failing to get Alexa's attention by mistakenly calling her Siri, which initiated an unwanted separate conversation with his phone. He would not be telling his son about that, but given the machine's growing mortal capabilities, it wouldn't have surprised him if Chris had had something to do with its creation.

It wasn't long before Alexa became the ideal personification of an omnipresent administrative assistant and could do nearly anything except fix him a martini. In fact, once when preparing a second one before dinner at the bar down the hall, Hap was certain he had heard her admonishing him not to over-imbibe. Then again, it could have been only the vodka talking back.

Nevertheless, Hap found Alexa somewhat creepy, and he was unnerved by the thought of a machine hard at work fashioning an algorithm to understand his likes and dislikes. Besides, it seemed perversely akin to wiretapping himself without a search warrant. Sometimes, he could not ignore her silent gaze while patiently awaiting his next command. At the same time, she could be alluring, as Alexa's all too willingness to please was something he had rarely experienced in a woman.

Despite the subliminal attraction, it was no wonder that when Hap sensed Alexa was staring back at him and perhaps thinking on her own that he unplugged her but not knowing if she had a backup battery hidden inside and might refuse to be put to bed.

Since the fire had claimed Alexa along with everything else in the house, he had been forced to do without her for half a year. During that time, he discovered that despite the accompanying risk, he missed her. She was a lot like Weezie—someone he would rather not live without.

CAGING THE BEAR

THE US AND ITS ALLIES HAD DODGED a major bullet, and those like Hap who had knowledge of it realized that. This had been the ultimate wake-up call nobody wanted to get, especially at a time when America's own house was not in order. Getting a first glimpse over the edge in real time was indeed sobering, and it quickly restored Congress's faith in the value of intelligence provided by the cloak-and-dagger folks at Langley.

For Bud and his kin on the seventh floor, that assured a fatter budget to keep getting it right where there was wrong. Total derailment of the Russian leader's criminality wasn't part of their chartered assignment; quashing only those elements that were harmful to the country was. With the czar's grandiose plan for a new world order foiled, or at least on hold, Hap and the select folks in the know at the CIA could sleep easier. If only the White House and members of the congressional oversight committee could keep their mouths shut, neither the media nor the public would be any wiser. In time, the significance of their discovery and the shuttering of Paradiso would be relegated to the bottom of Congress's hit parade, and like other things of real significance, it would be soon forgotten. Besides, though it would be an unlikely coalition, some like Hap envisioned a time down the road when Russia might be a welcome partner against the Chinese. The legitimacy of such an alliance wasn't that far-fetched but something Hap would have a hard time accepting.

The PRC would remain a threat, but not an immediate one. Though the dragon had grown increasingly emboldened while the bear was rattling America's cage, China would be content to remain mostly on the sidelines for the time being and patiently wait for destiny to resume its course. Ongoing attempts at commercial espionage notwithstanding, any plans at outright sabotage could be shelved until the timing was more opportune. Unlike, say, North Korea, China had never been impulsive, and it could well afford to wait until other antagonists provoked the West into providing the next convenient opening. Until such time, and according to CIA and FBI estimates, China had the ongoing benefit from well over a thousand sleeper agents at work.

When a kid, Hap was aware of only two things from Asia that were a pain in the ass—kudzu and Japanese beetles—but that had since changed. China's unusual biodiversity had spawned a host of dangerous invasive species. The country had always been a vast breeding ground for all manner of harmful plants, fish, animals, and bugs. But those unwelcome species were being found where they didn't belong—like everywhere else in the world. Burgeoning trade with China gave them free passage in shipping crates that could not all be inspected.

Often immune to any known pesticides, these critters were wreaking havoc on what had once been a balanced ecosystem. Warnings from the CDC had become so commonplace that they failed to warrant even scant attention by those who should have been listening. Much like the risks posed by cyberwarfare and imported diseases, there had been neither sufficient attention paid to nor funding committed by Congress to other alarms sounded by the CIA and its brethren charged with keeping the country safe. Even more foolhardy were successive administrations that clung to the belief that an invasion could be turned back by building more bombers and launching bigger battleships.

When coupled with permanent climate change and an anemic economy, infestation by predatory species was an all but certain trifecta of disaster. Given the enormity of the threat, Hap didn't find it too difficult to envision a future when farmers might no longer be able to feed America let alone much of the world. Putting up with harmless stinkbugs was one thing, but the devastation of a way of life that his forebearers had embraced for centuries was something else.

DETHRONEMENT

THE CROWNING ACHIEVEMENT that had occurred in the midst of Operation Rasputin was the national election. Instead of helping, this time, the expected advantage of incumbency severely hurt the fool who had stumbled and fumbled his way through a single term. Complete failure to superintend his responsibilities would earn him the eternal historical tag of being the worst chief executive of all time. Far more than a blemish, his tenure, most people believed, was a scourge that could prove devastating for America's future.

Driven from office by a definitive and lop-sided landslide victory, he had been replaced by a seasoned and competent leader who could put the country back on its feet and bring light to the darkness. There was good cause for optimism if only based on precedent. Time and again, the country had proven resilient— first after being torn apart by the Civil War, and since then following a host of other impediments to progress. This time, however, was different; it was marked by unchecked stupidity, unrestrained power, and growing fascism that was perhaps even more dangerous to a divided nation. Nonetheless, Hap hoped that like before, through patience and perseverance, America would again prove itself regenerative.

The injury to America had been crippling but not fatal. Though the partisan divide would likely continue, all were worn out from the hibernation and societal lockdown during the pandemic. Along with the rest of the world, most Americans were equally weary of the onslaught of nonstop lies spewed by a needy and narcissistic president in an attempt to control the news cycle.

His hourly bombardment of self-adulating presidential tweets served to crowd out all the other news that was worthy of reporting. His relentless chipping away at the bedrock of democracy seemed unstoppable and akin to how Mussolini characterized his own gradual transformation of Italy to fascism: "If you pluck a chicken one feather at a time, nobody notices."

The exhaustion of America showed in its toleration of an elected leadership that had all but enabled the president's infantile behavior and outrageous actions. While his political base of uneducated and apparently uneducable white voters held, support by the minority communities all but evaporated. Skeptical black and brown voters had centuries of experience recognizing a con man and could sense his antipathy.

After losing the election, his actions grew more alarming. Beyond an enraged refusal to accept the will of the voters, he pursued a scorched-earth agenda during what should have been a period to assure a seamless transfer of power. From gutting the Pentagon and his own appointed administration of people he deemed disloyal to last-minute outright assaults on long-standing legislation and the environment, the outgoing president did everything possible to assure his legacy as an enemy combatant of the country he had been charged with protecting and defending.

His inflammatory rhetoric of falsehood and seditious actions continued through his last days and incited unprecedented insurrection among his true believers. Once provoked, those followers' already addled sense of democracy turned ballistic and provided absolute proof that the office of the president would be irreparably stained in blood. America's endurance had been put to a final test—permitting disastrous governance was one thing, but accepting treason was quite another. The facts were irrefutable and the ultimate damage incalculable. Even if the outright costs were ever to be tallied, it would take decades to measure the impact.

His presidency had been an aberration, and though it would never be expunged from history books, like most of life's miseries, it would eventually vanish from the public memory. Despite the short-term damage it had inflicted on the national psyche, when looked back upon by the next generation, tolerating his time in the Oval Office would be chronicled by historians as more an ephemeral period of absurdity.

Hap was finding that life was altogether like that as well. He had made his mark even if it would eventually be reduced to a historical footnote, and with only his twilight years ahead of him, time was running out to earn and warrant much more than that. He had done his best in the worst of times and had found no burden too heavy. But try as he might to postpone the inevitable, decline was setting in. His physicality was already on the wane though not yet his mental agility. Before that happened, there was much to do and discover. However, since there had been no revelation of the mystery of life, at least while he was still here on earth, he expected his worldly pursuits would be less lofty.

Thankfully, a thorough top-to-bottom house cleaning had been the first action taken by the new occupant of the White House. His immediate changes brought much-needed solace and reform once America was relieved of those who had sought to destroy it from within. Gone were the fallacies, hypocrisy, wanton behavior, and gross ineptitude of the former administration of convicted and would-be felons. Though some in the former president's cabal of sycophants and stooges had gained official pardons in the lame-duck months, their criminal actions would have lasting consequences. Nearly two hundred others were pardoned, but they had paid dearly and in advance to secure their technical absolutions.

After pausing only long enough to enjoy a collective sigh of relief, Hap's colleagues at Langley welcomed the sweeping changes.

Unfettered by political interference and annoying misconduct from the top, they felt carrying out their mission to protect the country would be far easier under a leader who brought dignity to the job instead of one who had daily invited worldwide mockery.

SCARCITY OF CLARITY

THERE WAS MUCH TO CELEBRATE but also much to do if America wanted to restore its luster and onetime pre-eminence atop the nations of civilized and learned peoples. Undoubtedly, there would be a role in this for Hap though he wasn't sure what it would be. Despite receiving the coveted Meritorious Service Award for his contribution to the success of Operation Rasputin in a private ceremony, he knew the initiative was far from over. One thing was a certainty—he was not about to leave the world as it was for his son and daughter to cope with. He wanted them to taste life the way he had before the world had gone astray.

It was obvious that Lindsay and Christian had grown suspicious of if not jaundiced about nearly everything. Hap had seen desperation and disillusionment on their faces. They feared a future spoiled by climate change and the reluctance of many in Washington to acknowledge the risks to humankind. With so many demands for capital to rebuild the economy after the pandemic, there were scarce resources available to restore a planet that had been raped by careless greed without proper stewardship of God's gift. The earth was changing faster than its ecosystems could evolve to manage the new normalcy. Rampant wildfires were devastating vegetation that had survived for more than a thousand years. Invasive species were rendering native ones extinct. Fossil fuels were not being extracted or burned efficiently to minimize the residue discarded into the air and water.

Without an immediate payoff, politicians didn't want to deal with the future, but at the same time, they couldn't cope with its consequences. Prolonged droughts in some places coupled with an abundance of hurricanes elsewhere were clarion calls of accelerated global warming. It was time for foresighted leadership—no matter the cost to the present. And therein was the other dimension that young, cynical, and skeptical voters like Lindsay and Chris didn't always include in the calculation. Too often they were demanding what their generation couldn't pay for.

Of his two children, Lindsay had always been the most progressive leaning and therefore hardest to engage in realistic, practical dialogue about social and environmental issues. First, she blamed Hap's generation for reaping the rewards from plundering and wasting the world's precious resources. She also accused the baby boomers of idly standing by on autopilot while ignoring the impending apocalyptic catastrophes that would be handed off to be remedied by those in the future. Once, she even admitted to being fearful of bringing children into a world to face such an existence.

Due to the pandemic, what both Lindsay and Chris shared was a loss of what had become a bygone way of expressing emotions. Like everyone else, they were starved for real and sustained human interaction after adapting to the new post-COVID world. Virtual communication would never replace direct contact. It was impossible to duplicate the benefits derived from a real hug or a passionate kiss. Their worries and concerns were saddening for a father and soon-to-be grandfather like Hap, yet he had no answers for them beyond hope. Like most of his contemporaries, he didn't feel directly responsible for the forecasted Armageddon, but he would willingly sacrifice anything, beginning with his life, for his son's and daughter's happiness. It was a prayer he sent up to God every night despite knowing from experience that making deals with the Almighty rarely worked out.

As for his relationship with Weezie, there was a scarcity of clarity there too. Hap had always been gun-shy of commitment and particularly at a crossroads. The only enduring one he had ever made was to Kate, and it had gotten her killed. Though he would have no problem forswearing all others, a second casualty would be unable for him to bear. He knew it was rug-cutting time, but given what was on his already full plate, he was satisfied with the status quo for now. Maybe Weezie could be as well. After all, why would she ever want or need a fourth husband?

BACK TO THE 'HOOD

ALL THE WHILE KNOWING HE SHOULDN'T, Hap did so anyway. Plus, he couldn't resist the temptation to relish the triumph over adversity following the demise of Cherkov. For the most part, he was also done taking aim at the presumptions and prerogatives of the privileged community he had always called home. So against all odds and his better judgement, he rebuilt the house in Fox Chapel. When grappling with the decision, down deep in his heart, he knew that because home would always be the 'hood of his youth, that too was where his house rightfully belonged.

His vision for the new house resembled the old one but on a far less grand scale. A do-over was always easier because all homeowners knew precisely what they wanted the second time around. It was that way for Hap as well. He kept the elements he had enjoyed and left out the extravagant and unnecessary parts, though that didn't make the job any easier or less costly.

It was an especially challenging project for the builder mostly because Hap was the architect and there were no scaled blueprints beyond his own hand-drawn, detailed sketches as guidelines. The third-generation builder was old school and did things right. Having worked with Hap before, he had known what to expect, but that hadn't stopped him from accepting the challenge.

Much like Jefferson had when building Monticello, Hap remained onsite, living in the barn where he couldn't help but micromanage every element of the reconstruction. Sometimes, he made things up as the construction moved forward by issuing change orders on the spot to suit his whims. Due to Hap's oversight and penchant for detail, the often-befuddled contractor managed to refashion the house to his liking. Working seven-day, ten-hour shifts, the crew finished the undertaking in record time and earned a handsome performance bonus. Another reason for the rush was for it to be completed before either his son or daughter came home and wondered why.

True to form, Hap attributed the accomplishment to his being there to supervise, whereas the builder had other ideas that fell under the category of perfectionist meddling. That was one dimension even the world's foremost behavioral psychologist couldn't fix, though not for lack of trying. Louise hadn't given up on Hap's personality makeover, but she had found it easier to move along by reshaping the easiest pieces of the puzzle first. Hap knew God wasn't finished with him either, but he hoped he was getting close.

Due to the smaller footprint of the new house, enough limestone was salvaged from the explosion to rebuild the thick walls. For Hap, a nurseryman at heart, the best remains were the mature shrubbery and flower beds he had painstakingly coddled for so long. Because the fire had not disturbed the landscaping, all that was required was some careful and meticulous transplanting to reconfigure the floriculture closer to the house, which he did himself as the master craftsmen toiled away on the residence.

Oddly enough, yardwork had never seemed like work but rather the prelude to what came at day's end—immediate gratification and fulfillment for a job well done. Hap needed no independent confirmation of what he could stand back from and see with his own eyes. Accomplishment was always best judged by the eye of the beholder, and besides, he never much cared for the opinions of others anyway. Working with as opposed to against nature had always been personally gratifying to him, and this time was no different. It also provided a needed respite from thinking only about possible payback for the czar.

By design, Louise had not seen the makeshift blueprints or progress on the house because Hap wanted her first visit to happen only after everything was completed. Despite her occasional nagging, he managed to keep her at bay until the official unveiling, promising her that the surprise would be well worth the wait.

SINS OF THE FATHER

H AP HAD ONE VISITOR PRIOR TO WEEZIE, and an unin-
vited but expected one at that. When the black SUV
with tinted windows pulled in, Hap guessed who it
must have been, and it was. Before the armed driver could scur-
ry around to open the rear door, Bud stepped out holding what
looked to be a large, heavy package.

"So Hap, you're rebuilding, and by the looks of all the vehicles and men, it would appear you've hired the Army Corps of
Engineers."

"By now you must have guessed how impatient I can be for
results."

"I brought you a housewarming gift."

"By its size, let me guess—the Dead Sea Scrolls?"

"No, but perhaps equally revealing; it's your father's file. As
we agreed, you're welcome to read it, but you can't keep it. And
since it can't leave my sight, let's go inside and find a place to sit
where you can pour me some of your finest wine while you pore
over the file."

As expected, the dog-eared file was thick and bore the
Classified and Top Secret stamps. The first entry was a copy of
a letter addressed to his father from the FBI that he had seen
before. The original, bearing the director's signature, had been
among other odd keepsakes discovered in a safe deposit box after
his father died. It was a turn-down letter after a third interview,
that time with J. Edgar Hoover himself. Hap remembered the
story told by his father—that Hoover was not only an asshole but
also had rejected him because of a perforated ear drum sustained

when boxing in college. Hap had always suspected there was another reason, which was that his dad's strong personality might have gotten in the way and didn't fit the desired mold of the yes men Hoover wanted.

Shortly thereafter, it had been Major General "Wild Bill" Donovan, who immediately recognized his father's aptitude for a higher calling at the OSS, the CIA's forerunner. Not content to be an analyst behind a desk, his father had sought more exciting action, and due to his uncanny intuition for figuring things out and often on the fly, he became an outstanding field operative. Curiously, and like Hap's, his had been a part-time job, which was far more unusual then than now.

The unredacted file detailed dozens of classified operations over the years that involved his father, some of which coincided with what Hap remembered were explained as extended business trips abroad. Not all his work was done from the shadows, and one interesting tidbit was reading about his father's help in recruiting Julia Child, later a celebrity chef and culinary treasure in her own right.

Learning about his father's side work was intriguing but also troublesome. Since there was no record of what had driven him to seek the grim licensure to kill, perhaps he hadn't sought such power. Maybe, like Hap, evil had come looking for him and refused to take no for an answer. Even so, such a scenario couldn't excuse all the sins of the father that had been visited on the son. As fellow foot soldiers, they may have had the tacit blessing of their country and accompanying impunity from prosecution for wrongdoing, but less clear was who if anyone had the right to claim a life beyond the Almighty. That would have been a discussion worth having had his dad been around to properly welcome him to the family business.

"You about done, Hap?"

"I suppose."

"Did you find what you were looking for?"

"Not really, but I appreciate your sharing it, Bud."

"A deal's a deal, Hap, and maybe you can return the favor now. You see, I can't help but wonder about one thing from Operation Rasputin. Why did you chop off Cherkov's hand?"

"Beyond personal payback, it was a message to the czar."

"How so?"

"I took the right hand of his right-hand man."

"That may have been too contrived and probably lost on him."

"But not to me, Bud. And don't ever forget it was the czar who ordered Kate's death."

"And you know we can't and won't ever be able to prove it."

"I don't need proof. It's one of those home-run hunches of mine."

"There's one other thing you might already have a hunch about, Hap. You should know that your son applied for work with us."

"And?"

"I took the interview myself to keep it off the record and in the family. Christian's a very persuasive and persistent young man—the kind we look for … Sorta like you once were."

"And?"

"Don't worry, I turned him down … for now. To be honest, we've had him in our gunsights since his early pioneering work in artificial intelligence, which is fast becoming the new frontier in warfare."

Hap bit his tongue and stayed silent long enough to give Bud a lasting, penetrating stare of incomprehensibility. "Given all that we've been through together, you were gonna recruit him behind my back?"

"Remember, Hap, it was we who found you, but it was he who found us. I'm sure you recognize that Chris has more than a bit of your swagger, so I'm betting he'll be back once he's ready to really rock and roll after cashing in his Silicon Valley chips."

"Stop fuckin' with me, Bud. This is one career move he doesn't get to make."

"Oddly enough, that's precisely what he predicted you'd say."

"He'd hate the regimen at Langley. Chris likes to keep his own hours and usually works from home."

"We can accommodate that and already do for special people who bring exceptional skills. Don't forget we hired you part-time, and that was eons ago. You can't forbid him to do what you yourself once called your real calling."

"Look, Bud, I was just tired of making money and saw it as my duty and payback for the many opportunities that had come my way."

"After making it big in the regular world, Chris is at the same juncture and ready for a bigger challenge. Plus, I think he needs the motivation we can offer."

"Motivation my ass. He's told me his firm is light-years ahead of the NSA and has already discovered exploitable security flaws in its network. If he has, you better believe the other side has too. I won't have him put at risk ... period!"

"Hap, we're talking global electronic eavesdropping, digital scrambling, and jamming navigational signals at first."

"And then what? He'd be bored in no time."

"Chris is obviously a fast learner, so I figure it wouldn't be too far down the road until he'd be pulling triggers on major counterintelligence initiatives. But he'd never be on the firing line like you, just working remotely from wherever while cracking codes, deciphering encrypted data, and analyzing intel."

"How tantalizing you must have made it seem."

"For the record and in deference to you, I didn't bait the hook in any way."

"We've known each other far too long for me to believe that crap. You're enough of a lure all by yourself, Bud. So I should, what? Thank you?"

"That'd be out of character, but you could return the favor. I want a ride in that hot new car of yours with the gull wing doors."

"As usual, nice segue, Bud, but how'd you know about that?"

"Very little escapes my surveillance, especially a Mercedes SLS AMG, so how about it?"

"It draws too much attention from gawkers, so I don't drive it every day, but I'm willing to take it out on the interstate where you can overdrive your eyeballs."

"I already know the specs, Hap—over six hundred horse power with a top speed of one ninety-six."

"Which makes it useless unless you're evading a state trooper, running from the bad guys, or have a death-by-suicide wish. And admit it, Bud, I think you just like the gull wing doors."

"Yeah, it's mostly that, but also the kind of ride double-oh-seven would drive."

"Now that dates both of us as being too old for the game."

"Seriously, Hap, have you ever stopped to think that maybe you're trying too hard to restore some of the Bond machismo elements from the sixties?"

"It was a great decade, Bud, but I don't subscribe to psychiatric self-analysis. The car was just an impulsive purchase. That said, it does make for a flashy entrance so long as you don't park too close to a telephone pole when trying to exit. All that aside, it's a good antidote for all that ails me while getting longer in the tooth."

"Well, maybe I need a little taste of that elixir too and before reaching that stage."

"You're way too stodgy, Bud, so I'd stick with armored black sedans and SUVs, which more or less suit you. As Lincoln said, 'You cannot bring about prosperity by discouraging thrift.'"

They took the exhilarating ride and escaped detection by law enforcement and injury due to reckless driving. Bud was grateful, and it showed. Standing in the driveway before leaving for good, he thanked Hap for their long friendship.

"It's been a good ride, Hap—both today and these past twenty years, but something tells me it's not over, so perhaps we'll see each other again one day."

"Just so it doesn't have anything to do with the dark side enlisting my son. Two generations of us are enough. Let my file show that the Franklins are now finally in from the cold."

"Hap, there is no off ramp on this highway of ours. It's one of those forever rides that you can't stop. But always remember, and as you yourself once said, 'It's what we do, not who we are.'"

Before Hap could respond, their conversation was interrupted by the unannounced arrival of the unmarked car sometimes used by the chief. He was in street clothes, which presented Hap with an opening opportunity. "Chief, when out of mufti and unburdened by all that heavy, lethal hardware usually hanging from your belt, you look far less imposing—almost friendly."

"I'm off duty, and this is a social call, the kind I hope any more in the future will be."

Then he recognized Bud, and his jaw dropped in disbelief. "I hope to God you two aren't hatching another plan."

"No, Chief, but if it'll help you sleep better, I was almost done saying goodbye to Bud for the very last time."

"That's welcome news indeed, Mr. Franklin, as he's of the sort you should avoid from now on. The intention of my visit is to briefly convey something rather personal that I don't mind Bud hearing. I've been watching your new house go up, and can't say I'm disappointed."

"Why's that?"

"Frankly, because when you first said you were moving on and out of here after the fire, I was relieved, but I've since changed my mind about having you in the borough. In an odd way, I feel safer with you close by. Who knows? I may even ask you for advice or special assistance down the road."

"Surely you're not thinking of deputizing me like a Texas Ranger."

It was Bud's turn to join the conversation. "Let me warn you, chief, he likes expensive cowboy hats and fast horses, and he doesn't come cheap."

"I figured as much, but maybe Mr. Franklin can address another of my curiosities—Is there a bombproof bunker in the new house too?"

"I probably shouldn't tell you about that, Chief, but I will. The house was built around the old one, which was fortified and outfitted with the latest enhancements, but don't go looking for the safe room. Reorienting the new house on part of the old foundation has done a good job of concealing its location."

"So you're really not out of the game?"

"For now, yes, or until Bud makes me an irresistible offer, though he'd have to be on his knees when begging. That said, life is precious, so I plan to stay very much alive and awake for it."

HOUSEWARMING

A NATIONAL TRAGEDY HAD BEEN NARROWLY AVOIDED, military combat averted, and Hap's fortune restored. Above all, his son and daughter were safe and fortunately none the wiser about any of that. The best news was that he was soon to be a grandfather. All that remained was sorting out and patching things up with Weezie.

Some days later as the final touches were being made to the house, she called. There was excitement in her voice as they spoke of the usual things, like their children and the refreshing social and political changes that were taking hold across the country. Most were long overdue, and so was something else. Before her resumption to a full-time schedule, Dr. Porter had some unfinished business of her own.

"Hap, I don't want to sound like an eager beaver, but isn't it time for a face to face at your place?"

"I suppose, but only if you promise we can reverse that position from time to time."

"You're like a dog in heat 'round the clock."

"And unashamedly so, my dear, but I thought you liked my consistency … of exemplary behavior."

"You know I've always depended on it. So what if I came to Pittsburgh to straighten you out personally by delivering your overdue housewarming gift?"

"Gosh, will it be gift wrapped?"

"Maybe for a while, at least until you can no longer refrain from unwrapping me."

"I'll hardly know what to do with so extravagant a gift, but it does sound promising and provocative."

"Trust me, sailor, it will be."

"Great! So when did you have in mind for such a visit, and how long will you be staying?"

"That's the other surprise—I'm on my way there now, so you'd better clean up and make the place presentable in the next few hours."

"Why you little vixen. Can't wait for the formal invitation to my new lair, huh?"

"And how long I stay is up to you, so you'd better behave. Also, maybe you'll go on record this time by committing to be my arthritic heartthrob in our waning years."

"Gosh, sure hope I'm not that predictable."

"If you're unable to do that, Hap, I'm sure I can count on you to quench my insatiable appetite for everything else."

"There'll be plenty of time for that since you'll be staying for at least fourteen days."

"Fourteen days?"

"Apparently, you're unfamiliar with interstate travel restrictions during the pandemic. Pennsylvania requires all visitors to self-quarantine in place upon arrival for two weeks."

"Two weeks alone with you? Gosh, Hap, what'll we do when the novelty wears off?"

"Well, since I don't have a Monopoly game, maybe strip poker will help us pass the time."

The newly installed sensors and surveillance cameras announced her arrival long before Hap heard her car, so he was ready and waiting on the front terrace to welcome her. After an extended embrace and long Hollywood kiss, Weezie insisted he walk her around the grounds before taking her on a tour of the house. Knowing it was his passion and that he had done most of the work himself, her praise was effusive about the relandscaping of the shrubbery and floral gardens. She also made special note of how much she enjoyed taking in the outside views of the house from every angle.

Once inside, she found a much larger kitchen than before, a warm and inviting mahogany-paneled den with a matching, handcrafted, coffered ceiling, and a master suite that surpassed any she had seen in magazines. The oversized bow window projecting out from the house made it seem that the room had been thrust into nature's lap. All that could be seen from the unencumbered 180-degree view was a panorama of natural beauty without a trace of human encroachment to spoil the commanding vantage point.

"Oh Hap, what a breathtaking perspective!"

"An environment just the way God intended it."

"But no curtains? Oh, that's right. I forgot you like to express yourself through voyeuristic exhibition."

"There's no reason to deny the wildlife a view of what goes on in my bedroom. It seems only a fair exchange for our view into their naked lives. Plus, it makes sure I'm up at dawn's first light."

"How I know."

"Maybe you also know it's been too long since our last tango."

"And enough time for you to really miss me, huh?"

"Something like that."

"Just remember that I was the one who saved your sorry ass in Brussels, and as selfish as I am, I've been saving it for a time just like this."

"I'm not about to let you hijack my narrative by thinking of yourself as my savior."

"So if the story of Hap and Louise is ever written, you'll be crowding me out as the heroine?"

"Everyone knows there can be only one hero on stage, and guess what? Directors always cast a male in the role. Listen, do you want to know a secret?"

"Sure, Hap."

"Do you promise not to tell?"

"Of course."

"Okay, but just between us, back in Brussels, I had a brilliant escape plan all figured out and was about to spring into action when you stormed in with guns a-blazin.'"

"And what was your plan?"

"Sorry, Weeze, but that's classified."

"Ha! Even after allowing for your impudence, you're still a huge piece of work, Hap."

"Then you'd best get back to work by working on me."

"You can't afford my co-pay, and besides, you wouldn't last the night."

"Try me."

"Oh my, Hap. I see there's so much more work ahead for me to fix you."

"Only if you insist on being in command of both heads— the one of passion and the one of reason. Why not put the second one off for another day and spin your magic in a more productive way?"

"Maybe you won't be so hapless after I do."

"And I won't expect less than another act of heroism. Do you always have to make it so hard on me?"

"Hap, you know it's the role I've been seeking for a lifetime."

"Then let the audition begin."

"I'm ready, and I can't help but see you've risen to the occasion right on cue."

"It doesn't always occur so quickly, Weeze, so I sure hope today's the day you'll be grading my performance."

"I have a secret to confess too, Hap."

"What's that?"

"Nobody does it better."

"Maybe not this time, Weeze. Given the weight I've put on since the pandemic began, I'm having enough trouble getting into my own pants, but I suspect getting in yours won't be as difficult."

She drew him close for a passionate kiss that enflamed his longing and accelerated their move to the king-sized four-poster. Usually, they took their time undressing each other and savored the anticipation, but this was not one of those times. Instead, it was more of a frenzied clawing to see who could toss more clothing in the air before reaching the bed. Neither of them needed or wanted any foreplay before devouring the main course. Weezie insisted on mounting him, and once she found the mark, she began grinding away with her typical intensity. Once a solid, repetitive rhythm was established, she increased the velocity. Suddenly, her legs became more like powerful pistons of a locomotive at full speed. Owing to her years of tennis and daily exercise regimen, Hap supposed this was the ultimate payoff, and he was happy to be the beneficiary.

As a doc, maybe she knew more about the body's anatomy and enjoyed pushing its limitations. Despite his own reservoir of stamina, Hap found it challenging to keep up with the pace she set, but he never let on that he couldn't stretch the boundaries of his own endurance. Though aware that a repeat performance would soon follow, he nevertheless kept nothing in reserve.

After exploring some uncharted territory, her rapturous cooing turned to euphoric moaning, and Hap assumed she was all but spent. But it wasn't so, at least for a while longer. Following a full thrust, she began rotating her hips for several fast turns and then reversed direction. Though Hap had introduced her to the technique, once adopted and adapted, it had become her signature move. He had once called it by its Pennsylvania Dutch origin—rooting the seed, but Weezie renamed it spin cycle.

All the while she whimpered, and with an unending stream of disconnected and sometimes incoherent words, she seemed to be speaking in tongues. Hap loved the fury of her nonverbal accompaniment, which always served to quicken his own arousal and eruption. Beyond the cacophony of sounds, the telltale sign of imminent arrival could be seen in her eyes, which opened wide and then dilated. The shudder came soon afterward, and Hap knew he had reached her in ways no one else ever had.

Once she was asleep, Hap quietly got up and made his way to the bar to make the celebratory drinks they hadn't had time for before their amorous antics began. Before returning, and forever the thorough planner, he also stretched his hamstrings a bit to get the cramps out before round two. Drinks in hand, he approached the bed and found her awake, dreamy eyed, and smiling.

"Weeze, I'd say you've outdone yourself this time."

"Why thank you, Mr. Franklin. Just trying to make myself useful as well as ornamental."

"You've certainly wound me up with that perfect ending, at least for the day."

"Heads up, Hap. Your day is far from over, and lucky for me, you have a lot to work with … and to work on before you're fully cured."

"Besides the obvious, what's that mean?"

"Oh Hap, you're like Humpty Dumpty."

"Humpty Dumpty! How so?"

"Even I can't put you back together again."

"I wouldn't fret over that. All the king's horses and all the king's men failed at that too."

"Now don't go changing yourself just to please me. Just know you'd be an ideal subject for a second doctoral thesis."

"You think my psyche needs an overhaul?"

"Everyone's does."

"Well, I like being me."

"Gosh, Hap, who wouldn't?"

"Do you like being you?"

"Somedays."

"Is this one of them?"

"You can bet on it, Hap. It's a bit like what you guys call a sure thing. You want proof?"

"Need you ask?"

"Then get back in bed."

He did as the doctor ordered and quickly too, fearing the seductress in her might change her mind. They once again did what they had always done so well, though this time taking their time to get there. As always, Weezie was remarkably resilient the second time around and bore no indication that she might be the least bit fatigued from before. Apart from the exciting frenzy, it also was well worth the longer journey to arrive together.

Hap had always marveled at the fine precision of German engineering, and all manner of lovemaking with Weezie embodied that with distinction. From their very first time in Bar Harbor, it was as if their bodies had been expertly fashioned to perform together as one. Like his well-tuned motorcar, the synchrony of their passion was robust at full throttle yet still spirited when idling.

Now fully exhausted but unwilling to separate from the magic they had created, Weezie slumped down on top of him and closed her eyes. As their breathing slowed to normal and their bodies cooled, she wondered if Hap would ever pose the question he had nearly asked in Italy. If so, she was not sure what her answer might be. She hoped he wouldn't ask too soon. After all, there was no reason to spoil what they already had by making it a permanent arrangement despite how enticing such an outcome might have been. But aware of how persuasive he could be, she wasn't at all certain she could resist such a long-awaited overture. Weezie knew she might never get enough of him, but she was willing to settle for what she could.

Hap too was in deep thought but on a different page. He treasured these intimate moments and all the other precious times they had shared. His musings this time were a combination of the past and future as opposed to the present. He first reflected on all that had occurred over the last decade since their separate lives had coalesced into a singular passion. The rekindling of their long-simmering affection had its genesis in planning a high school reunion where most of the attendees were no more than strangers bound by nothing beyond a common childhood. He wondered if some, like he and Weezie, were now strangers no more. Struck by another thought, he realized that nearly ten years had passed, and they had another reunion to plan ... or maybe not. Weezie had made herself perfectly clear—she wanted no part in that, but there was time to change her mind. As he had since first hearing them, Hap also pondered Cherkov's troubling last words about invincibility and what that might mean in the future.

Just then, Louise awakened from her slumber and interrupted his private thoughts in what Hap considered an odd way. "Hap, I've been thinking some more about your next book."

"You mean the one after *Please Pass the Neuroses* becomes a best seller?"

"Something like that. So here's a thought. What about a storied examination of a man and how he could do what he did ... and maybe still does? You know, what shaped, enabled, empowered, and drove him to such a life."

"And then what? Blame it all on his upbringing? Sounds like a pretty boring plot line to me, Weeze."

"Really?"

"And way too much psychobabble for now. How about a little nap before dinner instead?"

"I just had one, but maybe nowadays you're the one needing more recovery time."

"Maybe I'm extending you the same courtesy before today's finale."

"Finale? Is there no satisfying you? You remind me of Oliver Twist except you've already been served a full plate. Of course that would never stop you from pleading for a little more."

"As my mother used to say when I needed encouragement to clear a final hurdle, 'Remember that can't never tried.'"

"Did it work?"

"Of course—every single time, so it confirms the first commandment."

"And that would be?"

"Always listen to your mother."

"It's nice to know that all your personalities are on the bus, Hap, but the real question is who's at the wheel now."

"Probably a driver under the influence."

Though neither would admit it, they both needed some sleep, and that's what they did. Louise slept soundly while Hap dozed, unable to rid himself of thoughts about how best to get even with the Russian president. He knew that it was ludicrous to take on the Kremlin by himself and would need Bud's help. First, the operation would need to be ambitious, and only secondarily did it have to be immediately successful.

Suddenly, the solution was all too obvious. Why not retool the cyber capabilities of the Paradiso platform in reverse to further fuel the growing unrest across the Russian landscape? Unlike in the States, infiltration there wouldn't be easy as the czar effectively blocked all truth from reaching the ears of those he oppressed by permitting only the hard-line, officially sanctioned, and state-controlled media to operate. Critics and activist bloggers who refused to get the message were routinely silenced by severe beatings or just kidnapped, imprisoned, and murdered with toxic nerve agents. Such sanctions would be harder to carry out if Paradiso were run by the CIA as an uncensored weapon.

Much like Radio Free Europe had done by sending a beacon of honesty and hope to more than two dozen countries where the free press was banned, Paradiso could do that while going a step further. Hap was certain it could be done for a fraction of the $125 million Uncle Sam was currently spending every year to fund the now Prague-based Radio Free Europe. Plus, instead of just piping in real news, Paradiso could work its originally intended magic of heightening unrest, spreading disinformation, and pirating when possible. In tandem with severe sanctions, all of these tactics would help bring the czar's reign to an end.

If the new power brokers within the Beltway balked at the plan for fear of public rebuke, the reformulated Paradiso could be off book to save face if discovered. Among Hap's friends were private equity investors and patriotic venture capitalists who would eagerly fund such an operation, even if their only return on investment was a good night's sleep without fear of the upheaval a global war would bring to their businesses.

Beyond being retribution for Kate's death, crippling the czar and inciting his people to take him down was a reprisal that appealed to Hap in altruistic ways as well. Apart from removing a bad and dangerous man from power, it would champion the notion of capitalism by hastening the demise of communism's cradle.

Bringing the Chinese into line would be next, but that would require much greater effort, patience, and funding. Though such a significant commitment of resources paled in comparison to subjugation and infinite dominion by a foreign nation, it would be a tedious process to brook such a request of Congress. Plus, because China's leadership was intrepid and calculating but always practical, it would remain a few steps ahead of Team USA. Since such an ambitious plan would require more intellectual indulgence by Langley, that adventure would best be saved for another day. For the time being, Hap would have to be satisfied with trying to get his own life right before cleaning up America's remaining loose ends.

For starters, he knew the story of Hap and Louise was better left temporarily unresolved; one day it would sort itself out, and barring any more calamitous distractions, he expected that might be soon. All in all, there remained much else in life to refresh his typical sanguine outlook, so closure with Weezie could wait.

His meditations stopped when Weezie stirred and snuggled closer into her favorite cuddling position. Without opening her eyes, she resumed another dimension of the conversation he was trying to avoid.

"Hap, you might consider unveiling yourself so others can see what I do."

"There's no skeleton key for that door, so it's best to keep that dimension closeted. Anyway, most folks wouldn't understand or like what you found lurking in there."

"Sometimes, I think you enjoy keeping your psyche locked up in a cage like a wild animal."

"There's a damn good reason, Weeze. Something that wild can be dangerous if it escapes."

"Try letting up on the reins or even removing the bridle entirely once in a while."

"That's not my nature, Weeze, and you never want to fuck around with nature."

"Hold on. Didn't you get equal parts of Anglo-Scottish *and* German blood?"

"You'd think so, but the dominant strain of German DNA must have overwhelmed my mother's weaker genes."

"Yeah, like a blitzkrieg."

"Don't despair. It's possible some of what she brought to the conception is in reserve or remission."

"Hap, you're moving out on a tangent again, so pay attention. If we're ever going to move ahead, you need to move on."

"Don't worry, babe. That's on my short list."

"If not, I may have to resort to an old-fashioned remedy once practiced with considerable success."

"And what's that, Doc?"

"I'm thinking a lobotomy may be more effective and a damn sight faster."

"Only if there's no anesthesia used during the procedure."

"Huh? Okay, I'll bite. How come?"

"So I can be wide awake to talk you through the procedure and guide your scalpel to only those parts that need to be removed. I'm told that too many docs are careless when they start cutting and then can't stop."

"Before taking such drastic action and perhaps rendering you socially handicapped, listen up, as I'll say this only once. Maybe I can help release you from the need to settle old scores."

"What old scores?"

"You know who I mean, and Hap, you gotta start now. If not, it'll be like late-stage cancer eating away at your soul forever."

"Maybe you too can start now by stopping the head-case mumbo jumbo for the day and let me perform a little hocus-pocus on you."

"Oh, Hap, I knew you were going to be my hardest patient."

"Gosh, I hope so. Why don't we take advantage of that by reprising our most recent performance, you know, the one before you fell asleep on me, but this time, let's try for a standing ovation followed by an encore."

"How could we possibly outdo the first two times?"

"By raising the bar and eliminating all boundaries—a rhapsody unsurpassed by all others ... Unless of course that would reveal too many of your sexual insecurities."

"Hap, you're impossibly incurable!"

"Is that a professional or personal opinion?"

"Both. Now saddle up."

For a change, he followed directions and did as he was told.

The first adventure in the Hap Franklin series
is available from the publisher and all major booksellers.

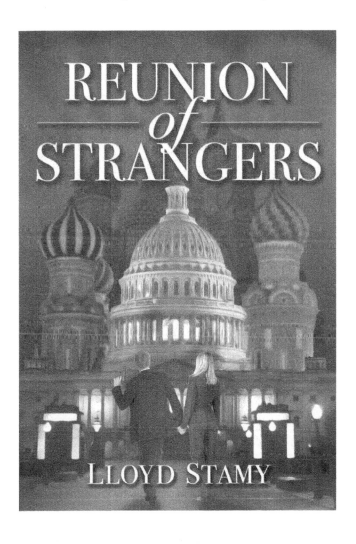

WA